A CHRISTMAS BETROTHAL

Obliged to seek shelter from the storm, Lord Ralph Didsbury diverts to a nearby house, closely followed by Lady Winterton and her two grand-daughters, Persephone and Aphrodite. But the house appears unoccupied, and when two further travel-weary gentlemen join the party, there is still no sign of the owner. Why is he hiding away? And are these young gentlemen who they purport to be? Ralph intends to find out, but as the appalling weather intensifies, so do his feelings for Persephone, and it is proving to be quite a distraction . . .

FENELLA J. MILLER

A
CHRISTMAS
BETROTHAL

Complete and Unabridged

LINFORD
Leicester

First published in Great Britain in 2019

First Linford Edition
published 2019

A catalogue record for this book is available
from the British Library.

ISBN 978–1–4448–4329–3

Published by
F. A. Thorpe (Publishing)
Anstey, Leicestershire

Set by Words & Graphics Ltd.
Anstey, Leicestershire
Printed and bound in Great Britain by
T. J. International Ltd., Padstow, Cornwall

This book is printed on acid-free paper

1

Lord Ralph Didsbury was slumped in an alcoholic stupor across the squabs, oblivious to the banging on the roof of his carriage. It lurched to a halt and then rocked violently. He was eventually roused when the door was flung open and a sheet of rain blew in and soaked him.

'Hell and damnation! What the devil is going on?'

'My lord, the weather is worsening. We cannot continue. The road is flooded ahead. We must find shelter immediately.'

Being doused in cold water had cleared Ralph's head somewhat. He pushed himself upright and wished he had not drunk so much the previous night.

'Is there any habitation close by?'

'There is a drive just ahead. I cannot see what sort of establishment lies at the other end, but if we do not wish to lose the team . . . '

'Take it. Whoever lives there can hardly turn us away in this appalling storm.' He resumed his place and the coachman slammed the door. The rain was torrential, icy, but at least it wasn't snowing. He should have stayed in town but his aunt was failing and his sister, Amelia, had begged him to come back to say his farewells. Milly had married the local squire, a love match, and he had not had the heart to refuse his consent. She resided near his own ancestral pile and was the only reason he spent time at home.

The fact that the Lord's name day was rapidly approaching was another reason to leave his townhouse. There was nothing he disliked more than garlands and decorations, false gaiety and festive celebrations. If he had remained he would have had no option but to attend a variety of parties: refusing invitations because he was leaving London to visit a sick relative could offend no one.

The carriage swayed alarmingly, taking the full force of the gale as it turned. He gripped the leather strap but still half-slid from the squabs. He turned the air blue as he heaved himself back into position. He was unpleasantly wet and becoming colder by the minute. The interior of the vehicle was as cold as outside — God knows how the unfortunate coachmen were dealing with the inclement conditions.

A full quarter of an hour later they arrived. He didn't wait for the door to be opened or for the steps to be let down, but opened the door himself and jumped out. He was almost lifted from his feet by a gust of wind.

'Take the horses to the stables and take care of them, and yourselves. I shall make myself known.' His shout was carried away by the wind but they must have heard as his carriage moved forward again.

The shutters on the inside of the windows were closed and there was not a glimmer of light shining through any of them. This was not a good sign. He hammered on the door and waited, dripping, for a response. Nothing. He banged again and this time he shouted too.

'I am Lord Didsbury. I am seeking shelter from the storm.'

This time someone answered his demand. 'I dare not let you in, my lord, the master would skin me alive if I opened this door.'

'I am likely to die from congestion of the lungs if I am kept out here much longer. I shall put matters right with your master, do not fear on that score.'

There was silence and for a horrible moment he thought the servant had abandoned him to the elements. Then he heard the scraping of bolts being drawn back and the large door moved a fraction. It was enough for him to ram his boot into the gap and prevent it from being closed again. He applied his considerable weight to the door and it flew back. There was a squeal and a thump from behind it.

He stepped in and was about to close it behind him when a flash of light from the driveway caught his attention. Good God! Another coach was approaching, presumably they too were seeking shelter as the road was now impassable.

The unfortunate servant girl was sitting on her backside staring at him as if he were an apparition. He was used to being the centre of attention — the combination of his unusual height and startlingly bright red hair was hard to miss.

He leaned down and offered his hand, the girl shrank back against the wall. 'I shall not harm you, child. I apologise if I knocked you over. Can you find your feet without my assistance?'

She nodded and scrambled up to vanish down a dark passageway. There was only one wall sconce lit in the cavernous entrance hall and the flickering light from this was not enough to illuminate the area. Most of the space was invisible in the darkness.

Ralph decided to wait where he was so he could open the door to the next arrivals as he was certain no one else would do so. He had yet to discover who was the owner of the property and why he was so averse to visitors. Despite the lack of lighting which might indicate the house was neglected, he could smell freshly polished boards and this was an indication that there was a housekeeper and a full complement of staff.

A house this size would require at least a dozen inside servants — a butler or at least a footman to open the door. He then realised the hall was warm so there must be a fire lit somewhere close by. There was no time to investigate this conundrum though; he was required as doorman for the new arrivals.

He positioned himself so he could see out through the slit he had left open and watched with interest as the occupants of the old-fashioned carriage descended to the turning circle. He could only see them because their carriage had lanterns swaying wildly from every corner.

It was impossible to discern the age of the three people who got out, but they were obviously female, that much he could tell. As they walked towards the house their cloaks flew out around them, reminding him of a trio of witches flying in — all they needed were broomsticks and pointed hats.

'Good afternoon, ladies, I am Lord Didsbury, a fellow traveller who has sought sanctuary here.' He stood back holding the door with difficulty and was relieved to be able to close it behind them.

'My word, young man, why have you not lit a few more candles. I am like to break my neck trying to walk about in the darkness.' The speaker was the shortest of the three, obviously a matron of considerable maturity.

'Grandmama, his lordship can hardly do that as he is also an unwanted guest.' The young lady who had

7

reprimanded her elderly relative dipped in a curtsy. 'I am Miss Winterton. This is my younger sister, and this my grandmother, Lady Winterton.'

He nodded politely. 'I am delighted to meet you all. I can tell you that we are not welcome here; it took an age for the servant girl to respond to my request to enter. I more or less barged my way in and the unfortunate girl promptly ran away once I was inside.'

Miss Winterton had removed her cloak and was shaking it out. 'I rather think, sir, the fact that you are the size of a small giant is what has upset her.' The girl had moved across to the one light and from that he could see she was tall, slender, had nondescript features and mouse-brown hair.

★   ★   ★

Persephone, better known to her family and friends as Seph, carefully untied the ribbon holding her grandmother's cloak in place. She was finding the presence of this red-headed gentleman a trifle alarming. Where on earth were the servants, the housekeeper, butler? Indeed, why were they standing about without assistance in the semi-darkness?

'Grandmama, if you will wait a moment I shall attempt to light some of the other sconces so we can at least see the place we have come to.' Her eyes had become accustomed to the gloom and she could see a faint glow from a fire at the far side of the hall. She handed the wet cloaks to her sister and ran across to investigate. There was an enormous basket of logs and a slightly smaller scuttle filled with sea coal.

Quickly she tore away a piece of bark and was about to hurry back to push it into the sconce when the sliver of wood was flicked from her fingers.

'Allow me, Miss Winterton. As you so kindly pointed out, I am tall enough to reach without the necessity of bringing over a chair.'

'Thank you, my lord, if we can see things it will be so much easier. Do you have your man with you?'

He spoke with his back to her as he was igniting the first of the sconces. 'I do not have a valet, I dislike being fussed over. You do not have a maid with you.'

She frowned. This was not a question but a statement — it was perfectly possible they had a plethora of maidservants who had remained inside the carriage. In fact, he was perfectly correct, they were travelling unaccompanied by servants apart from the two coachmen.

'You are correct, sir. My sister and I take care of our grandmother and have no need of assistance to take care of ourselves.' The fact that they could not afford to employ anyone even if they wished to was none of his business.

As light began to flood the space she could see that her elderly relative was looking decidedly poorly. Grandmama suffered from a weak heart and too much excitement could prove fatal to her.

'My lord, Lady Winterton is very unwell. Could I ask you to catch her before she falls? She needs to be warm and dry and resting.'

To give him his due, he did not cavil at her request. He scooped up her grandmama as if she weighed no more than a bag of feathers. 'We shall have to go in search of bedchambers for ourselves. We cannot venture upstairs without candles.'

Aphrodite, known as Dits, joined in the conversation. 'See, Seph, there are two on the mantelshelf. I shall light them for you.'

'Here, take my cloak as well and drape them all over the backs of those chairs. They should dry in here.'

With her skirts in one hand and a candlestick in the other she led the way up the imposing, carved oak stairway. There was no carpet on the treads but they were gleaming; they had been polished recently. There was a substantial gallery which overlooked the hall and three passageways led from it. One

11

straight ahead, one to the right and the other to the left.

'We shall go left, my lord. I think it more likely the central corridor will be the rooms for the family and the ones on either side for guests.'

'I shall follow you, Miss Winterton.' His remark ended on a gasp.

She knew at once what had transpired. 'Grandmama, do not stick your hatpin into his lordship. If you do it again I shall tell him he has my permission to drop you on the floor.'

'Too much shilly-shallying, my girl. Get a move on and find me a bedchamber.'

The first door opened into a pretty sitting room, the furniture was under holland covers, but there was no smell of damp and disuse. Once the fire was lit it would be perfect. She raced across and opened the door at the far end and as she'd hoped it led into a substantial bedchamber. The bed was already made up with fresh linen.

'If you would be so kind as to put

Lady Winterton on the *chaise longue*, my lord, she will do well enough there whilst we light the fire and so on.'

He did as she instructed but instead of striding away he shrugged off his saturated topcoat and dropped to his knees to push a lighted candle into the already laid fire. 'I shall do the same in the sitting room, Miss Winterton. Then I shall go in search of our luggage. I expect both your men and mine are languishing outside, unable to affect an entry.'

'Granddaughter, he is a very large man with difficult hair. He will not do for you, so do not get your heart set on him.'

Her cheeks were hot and her embarrassment was not helped by the fact that she heard him laughing in the next room.

There was little point in remonstrating with her relative as it did no good at all. She and her sister loved Grandmama despite her many faults and these unfortunate outbursts. When her parents had perished in a carriage accident, Papa's mother had taken them in, given them a good education and taught them how to behave in society.

Unfortunately, poor investments by both her father and grandfather had left the family with very little to live on. Therefore, whenever the opportunity arose, they accepted invitations to house parties with alacrity. Travelling so near to Christmas was not something she had wished to do, but if they had remained at home their meals would have been frugal and the house unpleasantly cold. The invitation to spend several weeks at the home of a maternal cousin had been a godsend.

'Seph, I have discovered a warming pan in the dressing room. I think there is sufficient hot coal in the fireplace to fill it.'

'Good girl, be careful not to burn yourself or to set the house on fire.'

'I am sharp-set, Persephone. You would do better finding the kitchen and fetching me something to eat than dithering about in here.'

She bit her lip and took several deep breaths before answering. 'I shall go in search of a servant, Grandmama, but I draw the line at stealing sustenance for us. We were not invited into this household, we are unwanted intruders and could be evicted at any moment.'

The old lady cackled. 'I should like to see them try, my girl, now we have that giant to take care of us.'

'Dits, I can hear movement from behind the panelling. I believe it must be our luggage coming to us along the servants' passage. I must find where the entrance for this apartment is or they could be wandering up and down forever.'

She took a candle and hurried into the dressing room. Her anxiety was misplaced. There was a door in there and someone knocked on it loudly as she approached. 'Please come in,' she called back.

Instead of the coachman she had

expected to bring their trunk it was the red-headed stranger. He dumped the enormous box on the floor with a thump.

'Your men have found sanctuary with the grooms who work here. Might I be allowed to come through to your sitting room, for we must talk?'

'Thank you for fetching this. And I do apologise for . . . '

He waved a hand the size of a dinner plate. 'Don't mention it. I am happy to oblige.'

* * *

Ralph couldn't prevent a wry smile at his words. Happy to oblige anyone apart from himself was usually the last thing he was. She gestured towards the bedchamber and he walked through as if he had every right to be there. The old lady actually smiled at him and he returned the gesture with a grin.

The younger sister had nut-brown hair, a pretty elfin face and a figure rounded in all the correct places. She was the beauty of the family.

'Well, my lord, what have you discovered below stairs? This appears a well-run establishment so where are all the servants today?'

'The explanation is not as mysterious as one might think. The master of this house occupies an apartment on the ground floor. He has his own staff, a private kitchen and the rest of the house is under covers. Once a week, women from the village come in and give the main house a thorough clean which is why everything is in good order.' He went to stand by the fire and warmed his hands. 'The girl who let us in had been sent to fetch something from the main kitchen and took the quickest route which led her through the hall.'

'Then it is a miracle we were able to get in at all. How fortuitous she happened to be there when you knocked. I am not, as a rule, a believer in divine intervention, I think we are on this earth to do the best we can without the help of any God. However, I must own I might have to rethink that after tonight.'

'I think you have not grasped the salient point, Miss Winterton. Unless either you or your sister are prepared to act as cook, there will be no food tonight or at any other time.'

Her smile made her look almost pretty. 'Fear not, Lord Didsbury, I am an excellent cook and as long as there is food in the larder I can prepare something palatable. I warn you it might well be cold as even if I am able to light the range it will not be hot enough to be of any use to us for an hour or two.'

'Tarnation take it! I do not expect you to deal with the range. Remain here, in the warm, and I shall take care of it. You have your trunk restored to you so you can find yourself something dry to wear before you venture to the kitchens.'

From her expression she did not take

kindly to being told what to do. With hindsight, it probably was inappropriate for a gentleman, especially one that was a complete stranger to her, to discuss anything so personal as changing clothes.

'I beg your pardon if I have offended you, Miss Winterton. I shall make myself scarce . . . '

'My lord, as we are on the subject of garments might I suggest that you find yourself a chamber and do the same? Not only are you mud-streaked, you're also leaving wet footprints everywhere you go.'

2

Ralph had yet to find himself a room and his box was waiting by the back door to be brought up. As there were no indoor servants he had no option but to do this himself. First he would select a bedchamber and light the fires — assuming that these had been laid as they were in the apartment the Wintertons were using.

The three of them could not possibly share one bed. Was there an adjoining room for the sisters? He could hardly go back and ask so it would be better to choose chambers as far away as possible from this one.

There were four available bedrooms and all in a state of readiness. The one that overlooked the gardens would do him very well. Within half an hour he had changed his garments, hung his drenched clothes over the back of chairs to dry, and had fires burning brightly in both his bedchamber and his sitting room.

His stomach rumbled loudly. It had been a devil of a long time since he had eaten. He would go to the kitchens and see about lighting the range. Cold food was all very well in the summer, but what he wanted was something hearty and hot. A jug of coffee would also be acceptable — but what would be even better were several glasses of brandy.

He found his way to the servants' quarters. These, as expected, were unoccupied but equally free of dust and dirt. As he was about to enter the kitchen itself he realised the sconces had been lit and he was walking about without recourse to his candle.

Miss Winterton was before him. He pushed open the door and was pleasantly surprised to find the large room was not freezing but almost warm. There was a large, scrubbed wooden table down the centre of the room and there were a dozen stools pushed under each side. There was no sign of the girl but he could hear movement coming from an open door at the far end of the room.

The range was hot to the touch and there was already a copper kettle sitting on the top. There was also a skillet warming up. However, there was no sign of anything edible to cook in it.

'Miss Winterton, I see you have lit the range successfully. Is there anything I can do for you?'

Her answer was muffled and he moved towards the doorway only to be met by her coming out, her arms laden with a variety of things. If he hadn't moved fast they would have ended up on the floor. He caught a basin of eggs in one hand and a jug of milk in the other.

Instead of being upset or offended by his sudden appearance she laughed. He rather liked the sound of it. 'My lord, thank goodness you were there as I am certain I would have dropped both items without your able assistance. The master of this establishment might have his own kitchen but he obviously doesn't have a pantry, scullery or root cellar at that end of the house.'

He glanced over her shoulder and his eyes widened at the largesse available to them. 'One man cannot possibly eat all that food and he was obviously not expecting visitors for the festive season. One can only surmise that the grooms and outside workers eat like kings at his expense.'

'I have fresh milk, butter, bread and cheese. I think if you are prepared to look you might well find both tea and coffee caddies in there. Could I ask you to investigate whilst I set about making us all an omelette?'

'Is there no ham you could fry to go with it?'

'Strangely, sir, there is no meat of any sort to be seen. You might well raise your eyebrows, I was equally perplexed. I am afraid that we must make do with what there is.'

He then noticed she had already set

out three trays with cutlery, crockery and so on. He would prefer to eat his food here and not carry it about the place so it would be cold when he finally sat down. He disliked eating on his own so would try and persuade her to join him after she had delivered the meal to her sister and grandmother.

She would have to return for her own tray as she could not possibly carry more than one at a time. If he set out a place for both of them at the table then she could hardly refuse to join him.

'I shall leave the repast in your capable hands and go in search of the items you mentioned.'

The room she had emerged from held the less perishable items but there was a second door which led to a slate-shelved larder. In here there should be sides of bacon, joints of beef, rabbits and pheasants hanging waiting to be eaten. There was nothing of that sort — just more eggs, milk, cheese and cream.

His search did indeed produce both

coffee and tea, also a cone of sugar and a freshly baked apple pie. Where had this come from? It had obviously not been baked in here or the range would have been hot. He could only presume someone from the village came up every day with baked goods.

'We will be eating the food meant for the owner of this establishment. I have fetched the pie and cream.'

She was busy at the range and there was already an appetising smell of toasting bread and omelettes wafting down the room. The kettle began to sing.

'There is a teapot on the dresser and a coffee jug in the cupboard underneath. I prefer coffee, but my sister and grandmother do not care for it. Would you kindly make us both?'

* * *

Since she had been obliged to dismiss the last of the staff a few months ago, Seph had taken over the duties of housekeeper and cook. Dits, bless her, was content to clean and tidy and take care of the laundry. The only luxury they had maintained was the ancient carriage, the two coachmen who were equally venerable, and the carriage horses. These, fortunately, were splendid animals and would go as well under saddle as in harness. Without the means to transport themselves to house parties they would surely starve.

When he reached out to pick up the kettle she called a warning but he ignored her and was apparently immune to the hot metal. He was a prodigiously large gentleman but for some reason she felt safe in his company.

There was a satisfying gurgling as he filled both the teapot and the jug with boiling water. She had made one large omelette and proceeded to cut it into five pieces. Two for him and one each for them. The bread had not been today's so she had toasted it and then put it into the oven with slices of cheese upon the top. This had now melted satisfactorily and smelt delicious.

With an expert flip she delivered the portions onto each waiting, already warmed, plate. Then the toasted bread with the melted cheese was put next to it.

'I shall take this tray up to my sister and grandmother. I shall be back for my own directly.' She had said this in the hope he would offer to bring it up for her but he merely waved a hand to acknowledge her remark.

Grandmama was now sitting up in bed looking a lot better. She delivered the food which was received with enthusiasm. 'Thank you so much, Seph, this is exactly what we needed. Do you mind if we eat before it gets cold?'

'No, Dits, you must eat immediately. I might as well have mine downstairs. I'm going in search of our unwilling host when I have eaten. I am not comfortable staying here without having met him.'

A sudden gust of wind rattled the shutters and the curtains moved. 'I thank the good Lord, Persephone, that we found this house. I'm certain we would have perished if we had remained outside a moment longer.'

'That is possibly correct, Grandmama, we are fortunate indeed to be here in the warm and not outside in this appalling weather.'

As she was running through the entrance hall she almost tripped over her feet when there was a thunderous knocking on the front door. Without thinking she went to open it. It was not her place to welcome in further stranded travellers, but there was ample room here and she could hardly leave whoever it was standing on the doorstep in this weather.

There was only one bolt to push back as Lord Didsbury had not bothered to put the other two across when he had closed the door after their arrival. She was about to open the door when it swung violently inwards knocking her from her feet. From her position on her derriere she viewed with considerable disfavour two pairs of mud-spattered boots.

Her eyes followed these upwards and saw they belonged to a pair of young gentlemen. 'I say, I do beg your pardon, ma'am, it was the wind you know, not us.' The speaker reached down and lifted her easily to her feet.

'I am unhurt, my dignity only was bruised by my fall. This is not my house: my sister, grandmother and I arrived as you did seeking shelter. One Lord Didsbury was here shortly before me. We have yet to meet the owner of the house.'

The two exchanged worried glances. 'I am Richard Defoe; this is my friend David Johnson. We were on our way to spend the festive season with my family when we discovered the road was flooded just ahead. This is the nearest house so we came here for shelter.'

She was about to answer when his lordship spoke authoritatively from behind her. 'Didsbury, at your service. Do you have luggage? A carriage or on horseback?'

Now she looked at the two more

closely she could see they were soaked to the skin, their many-caped riding coats dripping water in an ever-growing pool around their feet.

'Horseback, sir. We had a groom with us and he is taking care of the beasts.'

'Good, they will find excellent accommodation with the others above the stables. I suggest that you remove your outer garments. There is little point in asking if you have dry clothes to put on and I cannot loan you anything.'

Mr Defoe laughed genially. 'Good heavens! I should think not. We would both be swamped by anything of yours, my lord.'

She had no intention of standing here bandying words with these two whilst her food got cold in the kitchen. 'I shall leave you to direct these gentlemen to a bedchamber, my lord, I intend to eat my meal whilst it is still hot.' She smiled at the new arrivals. 'Once you are settled, find your way to the kitchen and I shall prepare you a meal also.'

What his lordship thought of her suggestion she gave him no time to say, but whisked away down the corridor and back to the kitchen. He had set out a place for her at the table. To her surprise he had placed her food at the back of the range so it was still relatively warm. His plate was empty so he had obviously eaten his food rapidly.

She poured herself a cup of coffee, ignored the sugar and cream, and sat down to eat.

* * *

Ralph shrugged. He did not enjoy being given orders, but he had no option but to obey them on this occasion. 'If you would care to follow me, gentlemen, I shall show you to an empty room. The fires are laid; all you have to do is light them.' He paused at the bottom of the grand staircase and pointed towards the narrow passageway that led to the kitchen. 'Take that corridor and you will come to the kitchens.'

He indicated which chambers were already occupied and then left them to it. It was not his concern that they had no dry clothes to put on. They were adults and perfectly capable of dealing with the situation for themselves. He was more interested in finding himself something else to eat. The omelette and melted cheese on toast was a fraction of what he usually ate.

On entering the kitchen he saw Miss Winterton devouring her own food. She looked up and waved but didn't speak as she had a mouthful.

'I thoroughly enjoyed the repast but I need something more substantial. Do I have your permission to raid the pantry on my own account?'

'You can do as you please, my lord, it is none of my business. There are at least two dozen eggs, a loaf of bread and a plum cake. Do you know how to make an omelette?'

'I have made several in my time. Are you suggesting that I cook for the new arrivals?'

She laughed. 'Actually, I was going to say that you must make yourself another one if you wish to. But as you are proficient in the culinary arts I shall leave you to feed Mr Johnson and Mr Defoe. I'm going in search of our reluctant host.'

She gathered up her used items of crockery and cutlery and took them through to the scullery before vanishing in a swirl of skirts. He did not ordinarily take much notice of the ensembles of young ladies, however he could not help but see her gown was sadly outmoded. Ladies now wore the waist of their gowns under their bosoms and hers was not. The cut and cloth were good, but the fact that she wore unfashionable attire could mean only one thing: her family were strapped for cash.

This was one thing he had never gone short of. He was an only child and had inherited from both his paternal and maternal grandparents as well as from his own father. He had the largest estate in Hertfordshire, another almost as grand in Derbyshire and half a dozen smaller properties in Essex and Suffolk. He also had a shipping line and money in the funds.

For some extraordinary reason he did not like the idea that the Wintertons were poor. How much would be enough to ensure that they could live in comfort and that both girls could find themselves suitable husbands? As he had never had to concern himself with matters of expenditure he was not sure if they would need ten thousand, fifteen thousand, or more. In the new year he would visit his lawyers and discuss the matter.

He had thought the toast with melted cheese quite delicious so he set about slicing up the remainder of the bread and the hunk of cheese. He whisked a dozen eggs, seasoned them well, and added a generous portion of butter to the skillet.

When Defoe and Johnson strolled in, looking almost as damp and bedraggled as they had before, he tipped the mixture into the pan.

'There is coffee and tea, gentlemen, help yourself.' The appetising smell of melting cheese was wafting from the oven.

'Jolly good, I am sharp-set. I would have thought the young lady would be doing the cooking for us,' Defoe said with a fatuous smile.

'Miss Winterton is not your servant, sir, and neither am I. In future you will have to prepare your own meals.' He had spoken more sharply than he intended.

'I beg your pardon, my lord, for speaking out of turn. No wish to cause offence,' Johnson said.

Ralph dished up the food, giving himself the same amount as them even though he had already eaten, and then joined them at the table.

'Tell me how you come to be riding about the countryside in this weather.'

The two exchanged glances. There was something a bit odd about the pair of them. On the surface they seemed genial, harmless young men but he had caught a glimpse of calculation, of a hardness in their expressions when they thought they were unobserved. Why had they not answered his question?

'Our carriage with our luggage has gone on ahead. It must have got through the flood. We both prefer to ride, cannot abide being shut up for hours. We were on our way to visit with Sir James and Lady Thornbury. Do you know them by any chance?'

'I do not. I was returning home for the festive season. Didsbury is no more than thirty miles from here so I'm hopeful when the rain stops and the river goes down I can continue my journey.'

'And the Wintertons? Are they acquaintances of yours, my lord?'

'No, Johnson, they are not. However, I now consider them under my protection.' What in God's name had made him say such a thing? It was tantamount to making a declaration of intent, of indicating he was meaning to make an offer for one or other of them.

The two young men made no reply but busied themselves eating. He finished first. He always did. He dropped his cutlery on his plate and pushed his chair back noisily. 'As I prepared your meal, gentlemen, I leave it to you to clear the table and wash the dishes.'

Not waiting for their response, he strolled out and went in search of the young lady they had been discussing. All he knew was that the owner of this substantial and well-maintained property was an elderly gentleman who suffered from some sort of ailment which kept him to his bed. The fact that the house was closed, that visitors were not welcome, made him think that the old gentleman had no family.

The wind was howling around the house, the rain sounded as if buckets of water were being tipped over the roof, it was unlikely any of them would be able to depart on the morrow. In fact, he rather thought they might be marooned here for the next week. He travelled this way frequently and once the river flooded the route usually remained impassable for a considerable time.

Being cooped up with strangers, without servants to do his bidding, should fill him with dismay. However, he was rather looking forward to the prospect and had not felt so enthused for years.

3

Seph made her way to the far side of the house. The apartment she was seeking was obviously not where the main reception rooms were so it had to be where she was heading. A tall-case clock struck six. Was it unpardonably late to be calling on their host?

There were closed double doors ahead of her. She could go no further in either direction so must suppose she had reached her destination. She knocked loudly on the door and half-expected to be ignored. There was immediately the sound of footsteps approaching — not a girl, but a man.

The left-hand side of the doors opened and an elderly man dressed entirely in black viewed her with displeasure.

'Good evening, I am Miss Winterton. My grandmother, Lady Winterton and

39

my sister Miss Aphrodite . . . '

'What do you want? The master . . . '

How dare he cut her off so rudely? She did the same to him.

'Be silent until you are told to speak. I wish to know the name of the gentleman whose house this is.'

The matter hung in the balance for a moment as the door began to close, and then opened again. 'Sir Jeremy Brewster.'

'Kindly inform Sir Jeremy that I shall be calling on him in the morning. You might also tell him that Lord Didsbury and two other gentlemen, I misremember their names, have been obliged to seek shelter under his roof.'

This was obviously news to him. 'The names of the other two, Miss Winterton. Could I ask you to please try and recall them?'

'One was called Deveau or Defoe, the other had a more mundane name. Johnson or Johnston.'

'The names are not familiar to me. I must tell you that you will be unable to leave here for a sennight. This estate and the grounds are on a hill, the surrounding land is far lower and the flood will have covered all of it by now.'

'If we are to remain here over the festive period, we shall need staff. Would Sir Jeremy have any objection if we find some locally?'

'There is a row of cottages behind the house. I should enquire there. Good night.' The door closed in her face. She was not sure if she could consider this a satisfactory conversation or not. There was something odd about the way his manservant had reacted when she had told him there were two further gentlemen staying at the house. There was nothing she could do about it now. She must return to the apartment she was sharing with her family and collect the tray.

On her entering the sitting room her sister jumped up, smiling. 'Grandmama ate well and is now sleeping. Fires are burning brightly in all the rooms including her bedchamber and I believe we have sufficient fuel to keep them going all night. Have you come for the tray?'

'I have. I have discovered a little about this place which I shall tell you now. I think, on consideration, it might be better to leave the tray here tonight.'

Dits listened to her without comment. 'So now there are three unknown gentlemen in this house. We cannot consider our grandmother a suitable chaperone as she might well not come downstairs whilst we are here. I think that means we must remain with her.'

'I think it is too late to consider the damage to our reputations. Anyway, as we do not move in society I hardly think it matters what we do. I have no intention of hiding away, and I don't think that you should either. It will be the Lord's name day in a week's time. We are not with our cousins, but at least we are somewhere warm and comfortable.'

'I shall not go down because the gentlemen will be obliged to call me

Miss Aphrodite. What possessed our parents to give us such outlandish names? If only we had a sensible middle name we could use that instead. I dislike being called Dits as well.'

'I'm not overfond of Persephone or Seph, but there is nothing we can do about it.' She thought for a moment and then smiled. 'I did not introduce us with our first names so why do we not adopt different given names?'

'I shall be Charlotte, I have always admired that name.'

'I shall be Eleanor, that was our mother's name. I can see no difficulty with this. Grandmama can continue to use our real names in the privacy of this apartment and no one will be any the wiser.'

'You do not need to use your name as you will be known as Miss Winterton. It is only I that need to dissemble. You must practice calling me Charlotte.'

'On second thoughts I think this will be very confusing and I am bound to get it wrong. Will you not reconsider your determination to be known as Charlotte?'

Her sister fixed her with a stern look. 'I am in future your younger sister Miss Charlotte Winterton. I shall brook no argument on that point.'

'I vow that if ever I am fortunate enough to become a parent I will not christen any child of mine with anything but the most ordinary of names.'

'I am going to retire, Seph — no, Eleanor, I am worn to the bone with all the travelling and upset. Do you wish me to put a bolster down the centre of the bed?'

'No, dearest, it is large enough for us to sleep together without difficulty. Good night, Charlotte.'

Her sister giggled and disappeared through the door on the right. The left-hand door led to the chamber their grandmother was occupying. She checked her ancient relative was sleeping peacefully and then banked up the fire.

As she was about to blow out the candles there was a bang on the door.

The noise so loud she believed her feet actually left the floor. She knew who this was. 'Lord Didsbury, go away, we have retired for the night. I shall speak to you in the morning.'

'I beg your pardon for disturbing you, but I wish to know if you managed to speak to the man who owns this place.'

With some reluctance she opened the door and then stepped aside to allow him to enter. She left the door wide, making it clear she was uncomfortable entertaining a gentleman in her private apartment.

She told him succinctly what she knew and then looked pointedly at the door. He misinterpreted her gesture and reached out and closed it. Her heart thudded uncomfortably. She had never been alone with a gentleman before this.

'You are right to be cautious, Miss Winterton. I believe that the new arrivals are not what they seem. There is something havey-cavey about them. I deduced from what you have told me that Sir Jeremy might well be hiding from something or someone. This is why the house appears deserted.'

'You think those two gentlemen might have been looking for him? Have come here deliberately for some reason?'

'I think it a distinct possibility. We have stumbled across something that has nothing to do with us.'

She swallowed a lump in her throat. His expression changed and he smiled. 'Do not look so worried, you will come to no harm whilst you are here. As Lady Winterton pointed out, I am a large gentleman and capable of taking care of all of you.'

'Thank you, my lord, but your size will be of no benefit if they have pistols.' No sooner had she spoken the words than she regretted them. She was about to apologise for her silliness but he nodded, his expression grim.

'I have pistols in the carriage and my coachmen have muskets. I can assure you that none of your family will be harmed.'

His impulse was to gather her close, hold her until she looked less worried, but he restrained himself. To even be in her sitting room unchaperoned was tantamount to making a declaration. He had managed to avoid predatory matrons with vacuous daughters for the past ten years and yet here he was putting himself in danger of being obliged to make this plain young woman an offer.

Her answer was unexpected. 'I have the same in mine. I am an expert shot, so between the two of us we should be able to deal with those gentlemen if needs be.'

'Forgive me, my dear. You are an original and I am lost for words.'

Her delightful laughter filled the room. 'Now that is untrue, sir, you have just spoken to me. Please, won't you be seated. I feel it only fair to tell you a little about ourselves as you have so kindly offered to be our protector for the time being.'

She gestured to a spindly chair but he shook his head. 'That would not hold my weight, I will be better on the sofa.' He accompanied his words by action.

This left her two choices. She could sit on the chair she had suggested he use or join him on the sofa. He was amused to watch the expression on her face as she came to a decision. She took the spindly chair.

'We are stuck here until after Christmas, possibly longer. We were expected at my cousin's house, but I think they will be relieved rather than worried at our non-appearance. We are, as you have no doubt gathered, poor relations and are obliged to drift from one house to another as we cannot afford to live in our own home for the entire year.'

'I am not expected anywhere. I was heading for my own estate so that I would avoid being invited to various festive events in town. Also, my great-aunt is about to kick the bucket so I am hoping to be able to bid her *bon voyage*. I do not enjoy frivolity or parties and I particularly abhor dancing of any sort.'

Her smile was infectious. 'I can understand that, my lord, I never dance but for a completely different reason to yours I suspect.' Her eyes twinkled. 'I am an appalling dancer, I might as well have two left feet, and any unfortunate gentleman obliged to partner me soon regrets his kind offer. Whereas you must be the centre of attention because of your majestic stature and superb russet hair.'

This was the first time anyone had complimented his abnormal size and extraordinary colouring. He found himself relaxing, enjoying her company in the way he had not enjoyed anyone else's, male or female, for years. 'I believe I could dance with you. Your lack of skill would be no problem as you could stand on my feet and no one would be any the wiser.'

'If we are to stay here for the next two weeks then we must ask my sister to play and you can demonstrate this extraordinary suggestion. Then . . . Di . . . Charlotte and I can exchange places. She is the opposite of me in every respect — she is beautiful, talented and can dance.'

'Fishing for compliments? She is certainly a lovely young lady, but you have a different kind of beauty — and I have never seen more lovely eyes than yours.'

She stared at him as if he was speaking in tongues. 'There is no need to do the pretty, my lord, but I do appreciate your kindness.'

He was on his feet and at her side before he had time to reconsider. He knelt beside her and stared earnestly at her. 'Your eyes are almost violet in colour. They are large, lustrous and reflect your soul.' He intended to place a gentle kiss on her brow, nothing passionate, just a gesture to show her she was indeed a desirable woman.

She tilted her head as he lowered his and his lips inadvertently brushed hers.

This was the lightest of touches but it ignited a passion inside him he had never felt before. He wanted to crush her against his chest and kiss her breathless, to tumble her into bed and make passionate love to her.

He surged to his feet. He bowed deeply. 'I beg your pardon, Miss Winterton, I did not intend for that to happen.'

Instead she was on her feet and looking at him earnestly. 'There is no need to apologise, sir, I have never been kissed by a gentleman before and it was a most enjoyable experience. However, I think it would be wise if you left before we misbehaved any further.'

Her hands were burning through his shirt. He was not a passionate man, had kept the occasional ladybird in town, but preferred his own company and that of his dogs and horses. He was having difficulty concentrating.

Slowly he backed away, putting a safe distance between them before he spoke. 'I am going, my dear, and I bid you good night.'

He closed the door firmly behind him and then leaned against it for a few moments to recover his equilibrium. He felt like a green boy: his palms were clammy, his heart thumping and his pulse racing. What the hell was going on? Why should this young woman make his head spin? What was so special about her? He returned to his own domain and prowled about the room trying to make sense of what had just happened. He was not a debaucher of innocence and yet if she had given him the slightest encouragement he might well have taken things to their natural conclusion. What sort of gentleman did that make him?

He scowled and punched his fist into his hand. Even thinking such thoughts made him the worst kind of man. He had said he would protect the Wintertons, and yet it would seem that the eldest girl needed protecting from him. He slumped onto the daybed and tried to think of the reasons why he was suddenly so besotted.

Miss Winterton — he did not even know her age, her first name — how could he be falling in love with her? She was certainly unique. In her favour was the fact that she was well above average height, came to his shoulder which few young ladies did. Her waist was tiny, her bosom satisfactorily rounded, her hair glossy with health and her eyes stunning. She was also intelligent, courageous and had a lively wit. Against her was the fact that her features were no more than pleasant, her hair a non-descript colour . . .

He could think of nothing else he did not like about her. His mouth curved and he stretched out his booted feet to the fire. Yesterday he had been his usual curmudgeonly self and now he was feeling happy. At least he thought what he was feeling was happiness — he could not remember ever being content before.

★   ★   ★

Seph resisted the temptation to bolt her bedchamber door. She had seen the desire in his eyes but was certain he would not do anything she did not like. As she settled down for the night, for the first time she was looking forward to the morrow.

Her sleep was dreamless and she woke feeling fresh and eager to start the day. She scrambled out of bed, leaving her sister to sleep and hurried to the shutters. There was no sound of lashing rain or howling winds — was it possible the storm had abated?

She frowned. It was unnaturally quiet. Her heart sunk. There could be only one reason for this silence. She opened the shutters as quietly as she could and sure enough the windowsill was piled high with snow. There were patterns of ice on the glass; not only had it snowed, it had also frozen. This meant that reaching the cottages might prove impossible.

She found herself the warmest and most serviceable gown she had, and the most unflattering. It might well be sensible to appear as unattractive as possible and not give a very handsome and strangely attractive red-headed gentleman any excuse to pursue her.

With her outside boots on, her candle lit, she hurried downstairs. The hall was icy. Obviously, the fire had gone out. Until they had located the whereabouts of the necessary fuel she would suggest they didn't have fires lit anywhere apart from the rooms they were using.

As she turned into the narrow passageway that led to the kitchens, his lordship spoke from close behind her, causing her to stop so suddenly her toes were crushed in the end of her boot. 'My lord, might I suggest that you announce your coming and do not creep up on a person and scare them half to death?'

His chuckle made her laugh with him. 'I seem to spend my time apologising to you. Despite my exaggerated size, I am light on my feet. I did not deliberately creep up on you.'

'I did not expect anyone else to be up so early. I heard the clock strike six as I came down. I thought to get the range going so we can have a hot breakfast. I am hoping there will be fresh yeast and flour so that I can make bread for the day.'

'I shall take care of the range whilst you do the other things. Once that is done I shall go in search of the coal and log store.'

'There must be some way for fetching it that does not require you to go outside. Have you seen how much snow has fallen?'

'I have indeed. This is proving to be a most eventful Christmas and we are still several days from the day itself.'

'Have you thought more about the two gentlemen? Are you still convinced they are not who they say?'

'My intention is to question their groom before they have come down. If it is possible I shall make my way to the cottages and try and persuade any womenfolk living there to come and work for us for the next two weeks. I can pay them handsomely . . . '

'I am not in a position to contribute, my lord.'

He said something extremely impolite under his breath. 'Miss Winterton, might I be permitted to use your given name, and then you can dispense with the formalities yourself? I am Ralph.' He raised an aristocratic eyebrow.

She hesitated. 'It is complicated. My sister's name is Aphrodite and mine is Persephone. Neither of us, as you can imagine, are pleased to be so called. Therefore, Dits wishes to be known as Charlotte and insisted that I must be called Eleanor.'

'Do you have a shortening for your name?'

'I do, it is Seph.'

'Then that is what I shall call you. I am prepared to call your sister Charlotte but refuse to use a false name for you.'

He stood up and brushed the ash from his hands and gave her a blinding smile. 'There, Seph, it is done and I can leave you to your domestic duties. I told the other two that they must fend for themselves in future. If they appear, I insist that you do not wait on them.'

It was her turn to raise an eyebrow at his dictatorial tone. 'I can hardly prepare food for us and let them go hungry. Hopefully you will return with sufficient staff to take care of us whilst we are here. When I have got the dough ready to rise I am going to investigate all the pantries, larders and cellars and see if I can find anything more substantial for you to eat. I cannot think that a diet of eggs and cheese will be to your liking.'

'As long as it is plentiful, I care not what I eat. I'm not overfond of elaborate dinners with rich foreign sauces.'

She could hear him banging about, searching for the coal cellar and log store whilst she kneaded the dough. Once this was safely in the bowl with a clean cloth across the top she put it at the back of the range to prove.

Hopefully her cloak would be dry by now. She would go and investigate as Ralph — even saying his name in her head seemed impertinent — would require his caped coat if he was to venture outside.

4

Ralph found the flight of stone steps that led to the fuel stores. It did not just give access to this, but to a maze of other cellars and store rooms. The wine cellar was an exciting discovery as it was well-stocked. He raised his lantern and walked along the racks examining the claret, champagne, brandy and sherry wine that was stored down there. He was about to pull out a couple of bottles but something gave him pause.

For the first time in many months, his head was clear and this was because he had not fallen drunk into bed the previous night. He decided he would remain abstemious — at least for the moment.

Something made him wish to follow the dank, dark passageway to its conclusion. He walked for half an hour and had still not come to the end. He must be well away from the house by now, but as this was not close to the coast he could have no notion why this should be. There could not be smugglers in this neighbourhood.

Perhaps it had been built in earlier times to allow Catholic priests to come and go without being arrested. The house itself must have been erected on the foundations of the original and the architects had decided to leave the underground rooms intact.

He turned and prepared to retrace his steps. Only then did it occur to him he could have become lost down here and nobody would have been able to find him. He had not turned either left nor right so should be in no danger of being entombed.

He was chilled to the bone and wished he had had the foresight to collect his riding coat. He emerged into one of the side rooms and headed immediately for the kitchen in the hope he could get warm before he went outside.

'There you are, I was becoming anxious when you did not reappear.' Seph handed him his almost dry coat and he shrugged it on gratefully. He told her what he had seen and she was suitably impressed. She handed him a pewter mug of coffee. He looked askance at it and she giggled.

'I thought you would need more than a delicate porcelain cup to warm you. I too have been successful in my search and have found an outside larder with hams and half a dozen rabbits, a brace of pheasants and what I think is a cockerel.'

He frowned at the thought that she would have to skin and gut these animals. It was not a task for a gently born lady. He was about to offer to do it for her when she appeared to read his mind. 'They are ready to be roasted, Ralph, someone has prepared them. I can only guess that the meat is for the use of the outside men.'

'I'm going to investigate as soon as I have drunk this coffee. It seems extraordinary to me that there are three kitchens in this place. I have never heard of outside men catering for themselves in this way. On my estate they come in to eat and my cook and kitchen staff feed them before the inside people eat.'

'But no doubt after you have been served.'

He grinned, enjoying her teasing. 'Actually, I insist that my servants eat before me. After all, they have work to do and I do not.'

'I have never met an aristocrat like you.' She nodded solemnly. 'To be honest, my knowledge of the aristocracy is rather limited so I do not have much to compare you with. However, I doubt that any other peer of the realm would do as you do.'

'I cannot abide being treated as if I was different from everybody else because of an accident of birth. Do not look so shocked. I am not a revolutionary. I am fortunate to be in this position and do everything in my power to ensure my people are well taken care of.'

'I am delighted to hear you say so. No doubt you take food parcels to the sick and needy as well?'

'Not personally, but I guarantee you will find no one within my estates living in anything but comfortable circumstances.'

'You are an example to us all, my lord, but I beg you be careful as your halo might well slip.'

He laughed with her and pretended to push this imaginary object straight. 'You are impertinent, miss, and I have no intention of remaining here to be insulted a moment longer.'

Not only was his coat dry, but she had also found from somewhere a large woollen muffler and mittens. He had his riding gloves and a beaver somewhere, but these were more practical.

Outside, the snow was swirling. His feet crunched on the several inches that had already fallen and he doubted he would be able to get to the cottages today. It wouldn't be light for another hour, but he was glad to hear voices coming from the stables.

Here the horses were kept in stalls in a long, brick barn rather than individual boxes. The area in front of the doors had already been swept clean and he had no difficulty opening the doors.

There were more than a dozen horses, well rugged and all looked happy to be there. Four grooms were busy mucking out and two stable lads were carting the dung away in wheelbarrows. There was no sign of his own men and this annoyed him. They should be looking after his horses, not sitting back and letting the resident grooms do their work.

Then one of the grooms saw him, he stopped, touched his forelock and grinned. 'Your men are repairing your carriage, my lord. You'll find them in the coach house. I'm head groom here, Fred Smith, at your service.'

'Do you have sufficient fodder to feed so many extra horses and food for the men?'

'We do, my lord. No one goes short here.'

Ralph was about to make his way to the coach house when he stopped. 'I don't suppose that there is a sledge here?'

'There is that, my lord. Them two in the end stalls are what pulls it. They ain't thoroughbreds, they can stand a bit of cold and snow.'

'Excellent. I want somebody to go to the cottages and fetch back as many women as are prepared to work inside for the next two weeks. They will be well recompensed for their trouble.'

'Right you are, my lord. I reckon there'll be ten or more, plus three lasses what could work as kitchen maids.'

'I would like you to arrange for them to be brought here as soon as possible. I am hoping there will be someone who can cook for us.'

'My missus used to be cook here before the master closed down the house. She'll be right glad to have her position back even if only for a week or two.'

Satisfied with his meeting, Ralph

made his way through the snow to the coach house. He had no interest in the repairs, what he wanted was information and the best place to get it was from his coachmen. Roper, the senior man, was more than a coachman, he was his eyes and ears and made sure his master returned home safely each night. Ralph also wanted his pistols, powder and shot. He was perhaps being overcautious, but better to be prepared than found wanting in an emergency.

★ ★ ★

'That was quite delicious, Persephone, you are an excellent cook. I just wish you did not have to involve yourself in such pastimes. Both of you should be . . . '

'Grandmama, please do not think about such things. As long as we are together, have food on the table and clothes on our back then I shall count it a good day. As you know I dislike snow above all things, but this time I own that I am pleased to see the countryside coated in white. It means we can remain here longer.'

Her sister had neatly stacked the dirty crockery on the tray and placed it by the door ready to be taken down. The sitting room was delightfully warm but she had just put the last of the logs on the fires and if they did not find more then the rooms would become cold.

There was a knock on the door and she called out that whoever it was should enter. Ralph shouldered his way in carrying a sack filled with logs over his shoulder. He looked decidedly unkempt and still had his outdoor garments on. His boots were coated with snow and no doubt he had left footprints throughout the house.

'You must be in need of these, Miss Winterton. Forgive me for appearing so dishevelled. I'm in the process of organising some of the outside men to take on the role of footmen. In future your fuel will be delivered by them.' He nodded at the trays. 'I shall take these down for you. I suggest that you remain up here for the present, ladies, it is both warmer and more convivial.'

Her sister and grandmother took this comment at face value but Seph knew he was referring to the other guests. 'I need to return to the kitchen in order to prepare luncheon and dinner for us all.'

'You do not, Miss Winterton, as a sledge has gone out already to acquire the necessary staff. I am reliably informed the cook who was here previously will be returning with them.'

'That is good news, my lord, but it begs the question as to where we are all going to eat in future. I have no wish to have these temporary servants running up and down stairs with trays all day. I am sure there must be a breakfast parlour we can utilise.'

His eyes narrowed. He did not like to be gainsaid. Then her grandmother spoke out.

'I shall remain up here, I cannot manage the stairs. However, I refuse to have you confined to this apartment as well. When the house is fully staffed you will go down, as befits your station, and eat in the dining room with the gentlemen.'

He nodded but said nothing and strode out, his back rigid with disapproval. Without stopping to think, she hurried after him.

'My lord, I need to talk to you. Please do not leave in high dudgeon.'

He turned to face her and for a second she regretted her impulsive decision to go after him. Then he raised his hands as if in surrender and treated her to one of his blinding smiles.

'Well, Persephone, what is it that you want?'

'First, please do not call me by my full name, I prefer Miss Winterton to that.'

'Agreed. Now, why have you waylaid me? Can you not see I am a man on a mission? I have not time to be bandying words with you.'

'Nor I with you. Nevertheless, it

would appear we are obliged to converse. What have you discovered that has made you so determined to keep us from mixing with those gentlemen?'

'Come with me, Seph, we can converse in private in my sitting room.'

'We shall do no such thing, it would be most improper of me to go into your sitting room.'

'I hardly think it matters, sweetheart, as we have already broken all the rules but as there are no members of the *ton* to make note of our misdemeanours we can continue to do as we please.'

She remained where she was. 'I believe, sir, you are forgetting my sister and grandmother. I know it is chilly out here, but there is a window seat at the far end of the passage where we can sit for a moment.'

He followed her ungraciously and her lips curved. She rather liked the thought that she was able to persuade him to her way of thinking when she was certain he was used to having his own way at all times.

71

'Oh dear! The cushions are damp . . . '

He stepped past her and tore the offending objects from the seat and then folded his long length onto the wooden surface. She had no option but to do the same.

'My coachmen have been making discreet enquiries not only about this place, but about Johnson and Defoe. The house has been closed up for two years. Before that, Sir Jeremy entertained and travelled widely. As far as I can gather he is not infirm, but hiding — from what, I have no idea.'

'And the two gentlemen, have they arrived here deliberately and not by chance?'

'I suspect so. The groom they have with them is a surly individual, close-lipped, and keeping himself apart so he cannot be questioned.'

'I wonder what happened two years ago? On a different topic entirely, do you really think that we will have inside staff at some point today?'

'They should be here this afternoon

so your domestic duties will be over. Two of the grooms and one of my men have agreed to put on livery, move inside and take on the duties of footmen. They are somewhere upstairs in the servants' bedchambers getting changed at this very moment.'

'I am going to see Sir Jeremy. I think I might gain entry more easily if you were with me.'

'Then we shall go together. Possibly I can persuade him to tell us why he has become a recluse.'

'Then I must inform my sibling of my plans. I also think I shall put on my pelisse as it is much colder than it was yesterday.'

'Indeed, my dear, it is. I wonder if that could be because the temperature has dropped and there are several inches of snow outside?'

She jumped to her feet and tried to give him a haughty stare. 'If there is one thing I cannot abide, my lord, it is to be made fun of. If I were a man and you were half your size I would consider drawing your cork.' This was a highly un-suitable thing to say: a gently bred young lady did not use such expressions.

He moved with remarkable elegance for such a big person and towered above her. 'And if I were not a gentleman and you were not a lady I should take you in my arms and kiss you breathless.'

He strolled off and she could hear him laughing to himself. Her cheeks were scarlet. She had only herself to blame as she had lowered the tone of the conversation by her remark. She could hardly return to the apartment looking so dis-composed so she remained at the window pretending she was admiring the vista and the snow.

Eventually her cheeks cooled and she returned to her family to give them the good news about the staff.

★ ★ ★

Ralph was still chuckling when he came face-to-face with the two gentlemen they had just been discussing. He nodded and they returned the gesture. 'Good morning, no doubt you have seen the change in the weather. Breakfast is ready in the kitchen but you will have to serve yourselves.'

'As long as it is as good as the food last night I am happy to do that, my lord. Do you know anything about our missing host? Do not you find it decidedly strange that the house is kept in readiness for visitors but there are no staff to receive them?' Defoe smiled but it did not reach his eyes.

'I know nothing of the matter and have no intention of enquiring. I have employed sufficient staff to cater for our needs whilst we are here and our reluctant host will not be out of pocket. Excuse me, I have business to attend to.'

They must think him touched in the attic to be striding off as if he owned the place. What possible business could he have in someone else's residence? Too late to repine. He would investigate the reception rooms, library and study and make sure the covers were off and the fires lit so they could be used later in the day.

He had told Roper, his man, to make sure all the fires had enough fuel to last the next twenty-four hours. There was certainly more than enough for the winter stored away in two of the cellars he had discovered beneath the house. Both these had access to the outside through a hatch which would make it easier for deliveries. It could also make it easier for anyone to get into the house clandestinely. The first thing he had done was check the bolts were securely across.

With Roper inside he was certain the two of them could deal with anything untoward that might happen. He was being as fanciful as a girl imagining dangers where there probably were none. He had not felt so energised for years, not since he had travelled to India when he was little more than a stripling.

He was lighting the fire in a small

drawing room, that he thought was probably used when there was no company, when he sensed he was being watched. He continued with his task and then slowly stood up. Standing behind him was an elderly man, his hair unruly, his clothes in disarray. He was holding a lantern even though it was broad daylight.

'Sir Jeremy, I am Lord Didsbury at your service.' He bowed and tried not to look alarming which was difficult as he was twice the size of the gentleman facing him.

'Quickly, come with me. I need to talk to you.'

The man touched the corner of a panel and it swung inwards. Ralph ducked through behind him and he heard the door click shut. This was a house of secrets; life could not get any more eventful.

Sir Jeremy led him through the darkness and then touched something above his head and light flooded into the narrow passage. They emerged into what must be his private apartment. The shutters were closed, not a glimmer of light came in from outside. Illumination was provided by numerous candles and the roaring fire.

'I am in danger of death, Lord Didsbury, and I wish to ask for your protection.'

'Sir Jeremy, I shall keep you safe whilst I am here. But once the weather has cleared I must be on my way so what will you do then?'

The old man wrung his hands. 'I knew they would find me one day. I should never have done it. I have regretted my actions ever since that day.'

Ralph was about to enquire exactly what had happened but he was given no opportunity. A man, presumably his valet, appeared behind him.

'Forgive me, sir, but I believe you wish to continue with your preparations for the day. I am sure that you do not wish to speak to Lord Didsbury as you are.'

'I beg your pardon, I beg your pardon, I should not have come to you as I am. Could I ask you to remain here until I am correctly dressed?'

'I shall go nowhere until we have spoken of what worries you, Sir Jeremy.'

5

Seph had been standing outside the double doors leading to Sir Jeremy's apartment for several minutes. Was no one coming to open the door? She knocked again and waited impatiently, but even the maid they had met the night before failed to appear.

She was about to leave when she was sure she heard Ralph's voice inside. How could he be in there before her? She banged more loudly and this time added a loud request to be let in.

A few moments later he opened the door. 'I suppose you had better come in, Miss Winterton, as I cannot leave you making a scene outside.'

He stepped aside and she stalked past. He really could be a most annoying gentleman. The doors opened into a spacious vestibule and then a further set of doors opened onto a sitting room.

She headed in that direction and didn't speak until she was safely inside and no one could insist that she left without picking her up and carrying her from the place.

'Lord Didsbury, how come you are here yet I didn't see you walk past? How did you get in?'

'Sir Jeremy fetched me himself. This place is riddled with secret passages.' He pointed to the panelling by the fireplace. 'The entrance is there. Shall I show you?'

She shuddered. 'No, that will not be necessary, thank you. I have a morbid fear of spiders and the dark, both of which would be found in abundance in such a place.'

'Our host has returned to his bedchamber. He was only half-dressed when he came for me.'

'What sort of man is he?' She listened with interest to his description and to what information he had gleaned so far. 'Then I am glad that I have arrived at this crucial moment. My life up until our arrival here has been tedious in the extreme — I cannot tell you how much I am enjoying the excitement.'

'I too am relishing this interlude. It looks as if it will be a most lively Christmas.'

'I had forgotten we are so close to the Lord's name day. For the first time since I was out of leading strings I shall be unable to attend a service on the day itself.'

'Saying your prayers of celebration in the privacy of your apartment will be more than adequate. If there is, which I doubt, a Supreme Being, I am certain he will be able to hear you just as well from there as from a pew in a freezing cold church.'

'I have never heard a gentleman, nay, anyone, admit that they had doubts about the existence of God. I do believe but sometimes doing so is difficult. Before my mother died she said that I needed to have faith that everything that happened did so for a reason, and she was going to a better place to join

Papa.' She stopped, unable to continue, and brushed away her tears.

'How old were you when this happened?' His voice was kind, sympathetic, not something she was accustomed to hearing from anyone.

'Three years ago, and my father had died the previous year. Grandmama, fortunately, was already in residence so there was no difficulty with us living unchaperoned. I have done my best to keep a roof over our heads and food on our table, but we are getting further and further into debt and it is only a matter of time before I have to sell our small estate in order to pay our creditors.'

Before he could answer, Sir Jeremy came in. He was now of tidy appearance, his hair neatly brushed and his clothes immaculate.

'Welcome to my house, Miss Winterton. I apologise for not greeting you in person yesterday. Please, will you not sit down so I can explain to you why things are arranged here in such a peculiar fashion?'

Once they were settled, he looked from her to Ralph as if assessing their ability to be trusted with his secret. 'Two years ago, I was living my life as any gentleman might: I travelled, spent time in town attending the most prestigious events and was generally received in all the important drawing rooms.'

She leaned forward in her chair, eager to hear what had happened to change this. She glanced at her companion and he too was alert and ready.

'I am a wealthy man, I have more money than I could spend in a lifetime. I was happily married but my beloved wife died in childbed and I never had the heart to try again. A distant cousin, Robert, will inherit the title and my money on my demise.'

His voice trailed away and he seemed lost in thought. She was about to prompt him when Ralph shook his head. A few moments later Sir Jeremy resumed his tale.

'Two years ago I thought it might be wise to make the acquaintance of my heir. To my horror I discovered he was a despicable fellow. I shall not give you the details as they are too shocking for the ears of a lady. I immediately went to my lawyers with the intention of cutting him out of my will. I can do nothing about him inheriting the title, but as the estates are not entailed I can do what I like with them.'

'Do you have other relatives who could benefit from your generosity?' She could not remain silent a moment longer. His constant pauses were most aggravating when she was so keen to know everything.

'Unfortunately, not. My dear departed wife was an only child, as I was. I wrote another will specifying that nothing will go to Robert under any circumstances. That my wealth must be used for charitable purposes.'

This time Ralph interrupted the silence. 'I cannot see how doing that would cause you to be hiding away here. What happened to change things? Did your erstwhile heir somehow discover he was no longer your beneficiary?'

'He did. A clerk at my lawyer's office attended the same dens of iniquity and informed him of the impending change. I have been unable to sign the documents as there was an immediate attempt on my life.'

★   ★   ★

'Do you think the two men who have arrived here just after we did are connected to this event?'

'I do indeed, my lord, although from their description I am certain neither of them is actually my distant cousin, but cronies of his sent to kill me.'

Seph was looking puzzled. 'Sir Jeremy, if the first attempt on your life took place two years ago, why have you not been able to sign the document since then? Surely this could have been posted to you and returned the same way?'

The old man nodded vigorously. 'You are quite right to mention this, Miss

Winterton. There has been no communication from my lawyers since that day. I have written several times but received no response. I fear that the clerk is intercepting the letters before they reach their destination.'

'I assume that you closed down your house and sent word to your neighbours that you were going abroad indefinitely when in fact you were secretly living in this apartment.'

'That is exactly what happened; and I have lived a quiet but safe life until yesterday.'

'I wonder why your secret should have come to light now, as you have remained undiscovered the past two years.'

'I have no idea, but now I am undone. I shall be murdered in my bed because I have not changed my will.'

This fiasco beggared belief. 'Then change your lawyers, Sir Jeremy. As soon as the weather improves I shall send by express to my own and arrange for one of them to visit you here and get it done. Then you will be safe from harm and can resume your normal life.'

The old man looked somewhat stunned by his brusque suggestion. Seph hurried over to him and knelt down and took his hands in hers. 'Sir Jeremy, even if those gentlemen have come from London they will do you no harm as Lord Didsbury is here to take care of you.' The man looked unconvinced. 'Good heavens, sir, look at the size of him — do you really think even two men would be a match for him?'

On cue Ralph stood up. He measured two and a half yards in his stocking feet, weighed as much as two ordinary gentlemen, and to make him even more fearsome, he had hair that would scare the fainthearted.

Her lovely eyes brimmed with amusement which made him feel even taller. Their host looked him up and down and then for the first time smiled. A poor effort, but an improvement on the terrified expression he had been wearing up till then.

'My man is acting as a footman; there are two more of your grooms doing the same. I am armed and so is he. I guarantee that if you are correct in your assumptions you will be safe until you can change that will.'

'For the first time since that dreadful day two years ago I can almost believe my nightmare is about to end; that I will be able to open the house and live a normal life once more.'

'Sir Jeremy, we have taken the liberty of employing women from the cottages to run the house whilst we are here. The surrounding land was flooded when the river overflowed because of the torrential rain and now there is almost a foot of snow. I think it likely it will be the new year before we can leave.'

He beamed and patted her hand. 'The longer that you can stay, Miss Winterton, the happier I shall be. In fact, I shall join you for dinner tonight, if you will permit me?'

'This is your house, sir. We are the intruders.'

'Pish and tosh, Miss Winterton, you are my most welcome guests. Can you persuade Lady Winterton to come down this evening as well as your sister? I shall send my own cook to assist in the kitchen. I have been consuming only vegetables and dairy products for the past two years as a form of penance for my sins.'

Ralph was tempted to ask exactly what these sins might be, but refrained. 'If you will excuse me, Sir Jeremy, I wish to speak to the gentlemen in question and see if I can discover whether they are indeed a threat to your well-being.'

He nodded to him, smiled at Seph and left them to their conversation. He had said that he had doubts about the existence of the Almighty but was beginning to suspect that the hand of God had indeed played a part in bringing them all together this Christmastide.

Then he dismissed the thought. There were millions of more deserving people in the world — why should a higher power take an interest in them?

His man staggered past with an

enormous basket overflowing with logs. He followed him to the drawing room, checked they were not being watched, and then closed the double doors.

'Roper, I have information for you.' He then proceeded to explain why the house had been shut up.

'I have my pistol primed and ready in the inside pocket of this coat, my lord. The other two are loyal to Sir Jeremy; I reckon it would help to involve them. Nothing untoward can happen if there are four of us and only two of them.'

'Do that, it makes sense to be prepared. Make damn sure that gun does not go off unexpectedly and shoot you through the foot.'

He left Roper to his duties and continued his search for Defoe and Johnson. They must be either outside or in their bedchamber as they were certainly not downstairs. The study fire was burning and the room warm enough to linger. He found paper, pen and ink and sat at the imposing desk to write the letter to his lawyers.

No doubt his sister would be disappointed at his non-arrival and his ancient aunt would have kicked the bucket by the time he was able to continue his journey.

There was nothing he could do about it. He would much prefer to be here spending time with the young woman he had . . . he had fallen in love with. He froze mid-sentence, too shocked by this astonishing revelation to move. He did not believe in romantic love. It was nonsense, for nincompoops who wrote poetry — not for sensible gentlemen like himself.

No, he must be mistaken. He wished to *make* love to her — but love her? Surely not. As he had no experience whatsoever in this area he had nothing to compare it with. He must have met a hundred or more young ladies over the past ten years, he recalled none of them. Yet if he closed his eyes right now, Seph's face was there in his mind.

Why should he be so afflicted so suddenly? He did not wish to be in love, it was damned inconvenient. Hopefully, like a head cold, it would be unpleasant for a week and then vanish, leaving him free of it. His dilemma was that he had no option but to spend time with her which would only increase his affliction. There was something about Persephone Winterton that had pierced his shell of indifference. It certainly was not her outstanding beauty as she was no more than passably pretty.

He closed his eyes and her image swam before him. She had something less obvious than a girl who might be called beautiful because of her regular features, lustrous hair and perfect figure. Seph had an inner beauty that shone from her eyes and this was far more compelling. His lips twitched. The fact that she had a delectable figure was a bonus, but not an essential.

This would not do — this would not do at all. He must not spend his time daydreaming about her. He had promised to keep Sir Jeremy safe and that must be his priority. In order to be able to do this, he had to find the young men who had got the old gentleman in such a pother.

After his fruitless search inside, he decided to venture out and see if they were in the stables. He was about to fetch his caped riding coat when he reconsidered. Chasing after them, if they were indeed the villains he suspected them to be, would just alert them. Better to remain relaxed, let them reveal themselves by their actions.

★　★　★

Seph spent a further half an hour with Sir Jeremy and the more she spoke to him the better she liked him. She had never had a grandfather — well, that was not strictly true. Everyone had grandfathers, but she had not known hers: they had died long before she was old enough to meet them.

She emerged from the apartment, well-satisfied with the visit and eager to tell her family of this exciting development.

The house was definitely warmer, and it would be perfectly safe for her grandmother to come down and sit in the drawing room rather than remain upstairs.

She stopped to admire some family portraits, two landscapes and a marble statue of naked cherubs which made her smile. Of course, the difference was that the shutters were now open, letting in the winter sunlight.

Sunlight? It must have stopped snowing. The best place to see this would be in the drawing room where there were full-length windows along the entire length that faced the garden.

'There you are, Persephone, I was about to send Aphrodite in search of you.'

'Grandmama, I was about to come up and fetch you.' There was no sign of her sister which was strange. 'Where is Charlotte? She should not be wandering about on her own when there are strange gentlemen in residence here.'

'She was sitting by the window reading. I believe she has found one of those silly romantic novels that she likes so much.'

'I shall find her, perhaps she has gone to the library to search for more reading material. Are you comfortable where you are? Do you wish me to fetch you a chocolate drink, or a jug of coffee?'

'You shall do no such thing. There will be servants here soon and I can wait until then. Find your sister, Granddaughter. You are right to be concerned about her wandering around on her own in the present circumstances.'

Seph was at the door when her grandmother spoke again. 'Of course, it is different for you as you are past your prime and so plain it is unlikely that any gentleman would look at you twice.'

She bit her lip. It was difficult to hear the truth put so plainly and so very loudly. Her head was down, she was not looking where she was going and walked right into something solid. She reeled backwards. Ralph's lightning reactions saved her from a nasty tumble.

6

Ralph had been crossing the hall when Lady Winterton had spoken so cruelly. He was at the doors as she rushed out straight into his arms.

'Do not listen to her, my love, she is talking nonsense. I can assure you that I have looked at you not just twice but a hundred times.' She remained rigid in his embrace. Gently he put a hand under her chin and tilted her head so she was looking up at him. 'I do not believe I have ever seen a more desirable woman than yourself. I would say categorically that you are at far greater risk than your sister.'

He had her full attention now. 'You are speaking nonsense, sir, but I thank you for your encouraging words. I am not blind, I look in the glass most days.'

He captured her waving hand and placed it over his heart. 'Feel that,

Seph, why do you think it is thundering like this?'

Her colour faded and then flooded back. She tried to snatch her hand away but he held it in place. How could he ever have thought her anything but beautiful? Her mouth was perfect, her nose even better and her eyes were beautiful.

He knew what he was about to do was wrong, but he could not help himself. Slowly he closed the gap between his mouth and hers. At first, he just rested his lips, applied no pressure, gave her the opportunity to push him away.

The hand that was about her waist felt her tension drain away. She swayed towards him and he was lost. He increased the pressure and she responded.

'Lord Didsbury, are we to congratulate you? I must assume that my sister is to become your wife.'

Seph attempted to put distance between them but he refused to release his hold. She looked at him, her face anguished, and the last of his reserve melted.

He ignored the outrage of her sibling

and continued to hold Seph's gaze. 'I was intending to make you an offer, but thought it better to leave it for at least another week to allow you time to get to know me better. I am an irascible fellow, I will make the worst possible husband, and I expect you to rapidly regret your decision if you do the honour of becoming my wife.'

Her smile unmanned him. 'I shall do no such thing . . . '

'Seph, have you run mad? Are you refusing to marry a lord, and a very handsome one at that?'

Again the strident tones of her younger sister interrupted them. How could he have considered this girl to be the prize?

'Charlotte, go away. I wish to speak to his lordship alone. What I do is none of your business and you would do well to remember that.' Her tone was pleasant but had an edge of steel and the girl turned and vanished. He noticed she did not go into the drawing room to join her grandmother. When he had met them yesterday he had thought this a small, impoverished but happy family. This was obviously not the case.

'Ralph, you would not have kissed me if I had not encouraged you. There is absolutely no necessity for you to feel yourself obliged to make me an offer. Good heavens! We have known each other for a few hours only — hardly sufficient time to decide we are suited to a lifetime in each other's company.'

One hand was still resting lightly on her waist, she had not shrugged it off, so all was not lost. 'I shall take your response not as an outright refusal. We cannot stand here talking, come with me to the study.'

Her laughter filled the hall. 'Sir Jeremy's study? I believe you are treating this house as if it was your own. Nevertheless, I shall accompany you as I have no wish to be given a bear-garden jaw by my grandmother.'

There were two leather armchairs on either side of the now roaring fire. He gestured to one and he took the other.

'Why did you not snap up my offer? Am I not the answer to your prayers? I can relieve you of the burden of providing for your family. By marrying me you will allow your sister to make her debut in London, she will be not only the most beautiful debutante but an heiress. Your garrulous relative will have her own apartment and staff to take care of her every wish. You will never have to . . .'

She raised her hands as if in surrender. 'Enough, Ralph, I have not been allowed to finish the sentence that I started a while ago. I was intending to say that if I did marry you I would never regret it and not that I was refusing your offer.'

'I detect a hesitancy in that sentence. Please, sweetheart, listen to what I have to say before you answer me. I am three and thirty, have never had the slightest inclination to become leg-shackled until yesterday. I have waited all my life to fall in love and . . .'

'You cannot possibly be in love with

me, you scarcely know me. I believe that what has happened is that for some extraordinary reason we find each other desirable. I apologise if my blunt speaking offends you, I might be innocent but I am not ignorant. Passion is all very well but it is not something upon which to base a marriage.'

This was an extraordinary conversation but he was enjoying every moment. 'Speaking as a man of experience, allow me to say that you are talking nonsense. Passion is exactly what a union should be based upon, the rest can come later.'

'I will not marry you but I believe I might like to become your mistress.'

* * *

His eyebrows vanished under his hair. Seph immediately regretted her immodest suggestion but there was little point in apologising, the damage was done. She lowered her eyes and waited for his scathing set-down to begin.

The next thing she knew she was

snatched from the chair and was being held aloft. His eyes blazed down at her. He took off towards the stairs, his intention plain. He had taken her at her word and was carrying her to his bedchamber to do as she had suggested.

'No, no, put me down this instant, sir. I was jesting. I do not want to be your mistress.'

They were now halfway up the staircase. She had expected to be replaced on her feet but he ignored her frantic struggles and continued. However, instead of striding to his rooms he shouldered his way into hers.

There he released her so suddenly she fell onto her knees. He reached down and lifted her up. 'I am sorely tempted to put you across my knee, young lady. You will remain in your room in disgrace until I give you leave to come out.'

She was not often speechless but being spoken to as if she were a child caused her to stare at him, unable to utter a word. Then righteous indignation coursed through her.

'How dare you speak to me like that? You are not my father, my guardian, or in fact anything at all to me. Get out of my way, I am going downstairs to join my family in the drawing room.'

She had completely forgotten the reason he had been so angry with her. He remained firmly in her way, staring down at her, his expression far from friendly.

Her hand rose of its own volition, her intention to push him out of the way. His eyes narrowed and she hastily dropped it to her side. This was not going at all well and it was entirely her fault.

'If I apologise for my appalling suggestion, might I be allowed to leave this room?'

He continued to look at her with disapproval and made no response apart from staying exactly where he was — in her way.

She had been in charge of the family

for three years, had made decisions for herself and them and yet this stranger had the temerity to think he could tell her what to do.

'You would get your comeuppance, my lord, if I held you to your offer and married you.'

'Excellent, then I shall consider us to be betrothed. I think May would be the perfect time for the ceremony, do you not agree?'

She stamped her foot, not something she had done since she was a child. 'You will do no such thing. I did not say I would marry you. We would be constantly at daggers drawn.'

His arms were so long he was able to reach out and pluck her from her feet as if she weighed no more than a bag of feathers. 'My darling, I cannot imagine anything better than spending my days arguing and my nights making love.'

At this point she should have protested, have struggled, screamed for help but she did none of these. As soon as he touched her she was no longer able to think coherently, all she wanted to do was have his arms around her and feel his lips on her skin.

His huge hands moved down her back, sending ripples of delight wherever they touched. Heat travelled around her body and settled in her nether regions. She tilted her face and he obliged by closing her mouth with his. It was he that called a halt before things moved to the inevitable conclusion.

'Enough. I will not pre-empt our wedding day. Are you in agreement that we have no option but to be wed as soon as possible?'

She sighed and rested her hot cheeks against his chest. 'We have overstepped the bounds of propriety so comprehensively I should not be comfortable if we did not get married.'

'I think it might be wise if we kept this to ourselves at least until after Christmas Day. If we are astounded that we have come to this decision within a few hours of meeting each other, imagine what your redoubtable grandmother and sister will say on the subject?'

'I fear that horse has bolted.' She smiled at him. 'You are overfond of issuing orders, my lord, that is something you must curb if you wish our relationship to be harmonious. I do not take kindly to being told what to do.'

His smile was wicked. Being in her sitting room alone with him was most unwise. She attempted to dodge past him but somehow, despite his bulk, he moved fast and was always in her way.

'Then in future I shall use a different sort of persuasion.' His voice was smooth, like silk rubbing against her skin.

For a second time that morning they were interrupted by her sister. 'Seph, Grandmama insists that you come down to speak to her immediately.'

Ralph somehow managed to put his arm around her waist so that they turned to face Dits — Charlotte — together. 'Your sister has agreed to marry me. You may be the first to congratulate us. No doubt you have already informed your chaperone.'

'How could I not? If there had been a kissing bough made from mistletoe hanging above your heads I might have been less shocked. Seph, how could you behave so badly? You have compromised yourself and Lord Didsbury so he has no option but to — '

'I think you have said more than enough on a subject that does not concern you, miss. Might I remind you that when your sister becomes my wife, I become your guardian? I am not overfond of impertinent young ladies.'

Seph held her breath, knowing what was coming. Instead of being cowed by his reprimand, her sister fixed him with a basilisk stare.

'And I, Lord Didsbury, am not partial to overbearing, overlarge, obnoxious aristocrats.' Charlotte smiled sweetly, curtsied as if to royalty and walked away with her head held high.

'Well! I see I have not just taken on

one outspoken young lady, but two. I have never received such a thorough put-down and I must say I rather enjoyed the experience.'

'We are an outspoken trio; I fear it is the fault of our grandmother. We follow where she leads.'

'I think it might well be the fact that you have never been forced to attend the insipid parties, balls and routs put on for debutantes where they are all obliged to follow the rules or be ostracised.'

'I think you have the right of it, Ralph, we've never had to conform. I do hope you are not a conventional gentleman. You certainly do not look like one.'

'I have no time for such things. I think in the circumstances it might be better if we held Charlotte's come-out ball at Didsbury Court. I have dozens of grand neighbours who will be only too happy to parade their sons for her inspection. I had not thought to ask: how old are you and your sister?'

'I am one and twenty, I had my majority last May. Charlotte will be eighteen years of age on her next anniversary in April. In case you wish to know, my grandmother has reached the grand age of four score years.'

'I have a sister, Amelia. She is ten years my junior and happily married last year to the local squire. The only other relative I have is my Great-Aunt Jemima who is, I think, the same age as Lady Winterton. Although I doubt she is still with us as I was on my way to pay my last respects when I was marooned here.'

He offered his arm and she put hers through it. For the first time in her life she was pleased to be so tall as it meant that her head came up to his shoulder.

'If you would prefer me to, then I am prepared to do the talking for us. I cannot like her; she treats you abominably and what she said earlier was not only untrue, it was unkind.'

'I am immune to her spite, but I must own it will be far easier to have you by my side in future. She has always been impressed by the aristocracy so you start with an advantage.'

'You have yet to ask me what your future home is like, whether I am as impecunious as yourself, are you not curious?'

'You cannot be as poor as we are, very few people are. I believe that you said you would take care of us and that is good enough for me. You also mentioned that Charlotte will now be an heiress. Are you very rich?'

His smile curled her toes. 'I am indeed as rich as Croesus. You will want for nothing in future.'

'I have all I want beside me. I cannot say with absolute certainty that I would have agreed to marry you had you been totally without funds, but I rather think I might have.'

He raised her hand and kissed her knuckles. His eyes were dark with passion, but also with something else which she recognised as love. She blinked back tears. He deserved to have his feelings reciprocated but what she felt for him was not the same. Mutual desire would have to suffice. She would make him the best possible wife and he would never hear from her that she did not feel the same way.

7

Ralph could not have been happier. Now he had something to live for, apart from doing his duty to his estates. He smiled fondly at his beloved. If they were married in the spring, was it possible that this time next year he would have a child of his own? Filling his nursery had never been something that appealed to him but now everything was different.

His future relatives were sitting bolt upright together on the sofa. Charlotte, he realised belatedly, was the image of her grandmother and appeared to share her opinion on his betrothal to her sister.

He nodded politely to them both. 'No doubt you are already aware of our good news. Seph has made me the happiest of men and we are engaged to be married. I am sure, Lady Winterton, that you are as delighted as I am by this news.'

'I believe that you have no choice in the matter, my lord. It is hardly a cause for celebration that you have ruined my granddaughter's reputation and are now obliged to marry her to put that right.'

'Grandmama, unless you curb your tongue you will find yourself remaining with my sister and not joining us at Didsbury Court.'

The old lady surged to her feet and banged her ebony cane loudly on the floor. 'You will apologise at once, my girl, for your impertinence. I will not be spoken to like that.'

He sensed that Seph was about to say something that she might well regret. 'Madam, I think that you will find it is you that owe my future wife an apology. Charlotte, you must decide whether you wish to remain with your grand-mother at your old home or come with us when we leave here.'

'Are we not to go back to the manor?

I am not sure that residing with you before we are married would be a sensible thing to do in the circumstances.'

'Devil take it! I have not taken leave of my senses. You will live with my sister and her husband until we marry. She lives no more than a mile from Didsbury and will be delighted to have you with her.'

Her smile was quizzical. 'I am not sure that you can say that with such authority without having consulted with her on the matter, Ralph. However, I shall be delighted not to have to return to the dilapidated building I have been obliged to occupy all my life.'

The cane was banged on the floor again. 'Your sister and I shall accompany you, Persephone. Therefore, sir, my girls will be adequately chaperoned and can reside under your roof without occasioning disapproval from the neighbours.'

'Then the matter is settled.' He winked at Seph and she hid her smile behind her hand. 'Have either of you seen Johnson or Defoe?'

'They certainly have not been in here, young man. I might be decrepit but I am not blind.'

'Sweetheart, I must find them. Will you remain here until I return?'

She nodded. 'I shall be here.'

As he strode away he could hear the younger girl chattering excitedly and was confident things would move on the way he wanted them to. Even his sister, the most devoted of siblings, was going to find his betrothal to a young lady he had known for one short day hard to credit.

Downstairs, the servants' quarters were fully occupied. The sledge had returned with what looked like a dozen or more females of varying ages. They were in the process of divesting themselves of their clogs and cloaks and hanging them on the pegs by the door that led into the yard.

His appearance sent a ripple of what could only be apprehension around the group. He was accustomed to this reaction and stopped several yards from them.

'Excellent, I am glad that you have arrived so promptly. Which of you is the cook and which the housekeeper?'

Two women of middle years stepped forward and curtsied nervously.

'I am Betty Smith, my lord. My husband is head groom here and my son a stableboy. I was cook here until two years ago and I am right glad to be back, I can tell you.'

The second also curtsied. 'I am Mrs Hopkins, my lord, I was housekeeper here before being let go.' She turned and beckoned two girls, one little more than a child. 'These are my daughters, Sally and Mary. They will be working the kitchen.'

One by one the women introduced themselves and all, apart from two, had been previously employed here so would know exactly what was required of them.

'Hopkins, I shall leave everything in

your capable hands. I came down here in search of the two gentlemen who are also temporary guests. Have any of you seen them, either inside or out?'

One of the new girls stepped forward. 'Beggin' your pardon, my lord, but they were in the stables when we arrived, talking to a groom.'

'Thank you.'

Society would consider him foolish to thank his staff but he stood on no ceremony where they were concerned. He did not believe, as others in his position did, that just because he had been born into wealth and title he was somehow better than those less fortunate.

He was not a revolutionary by any means, but he was certainly a philanthropist and used his wealth to benefit those in want. The fact that his vast ancestral home was always fully staffed, that the grounds, stables and kennels were also permanently at the ready for his return was not vanity. By so doing, he was giving a hundred souls employment rather than charity.

Yesterday he had been seriously thinking of raising a company of men, equipping them and taking them to join the British Army fighting the French in Spain. He did not relish the thought of fighting, of killing, but it would have been supporting King and Country and given him something worthwhile with which to fill his time.

Now all that had changed. He would no longer rattle about his home on his own but have a wife, a sister and grandmother-in-law and hopefully, over the years, a nursery full of children. He was about to step out into the snow but decided it would be unwise to venture forth without his coat which was, if he recalled correctly, draped over the back of a chair in the hall.

The garment was not where he had left it. He muttered something impolite under his breath.

'My lord, I have your coat here. I was about to take it to your apartment.' One of the footmen was holding it out to him.

Ralph swirled it around his shoulders and buttoned it about his neck. He was unsurprised to be given his muffler and gloves. These had not been in the hall so the footman must have fetched them.

He smiled his thanks. 'Is there a side door, one Sir Jeremy would use when going to the stables?'

'I shall show you, my lord.'

The weather had worsened again and snow was falling heavily — they would be obliged to remain here at least until it had thawed and possibly longer. He would have to enquire from Sir Jeremy how long the floods would take to subside so the road would be open again.

★   ★   ★

'Oh, Seph, I cannot believe you have agreed to marry a gentleman on so short an acquaintance.'

'It was a *coup de foudre*, Charlotte . . . '

'Why are you addressing your sister by that name? I will not have it. She is Aphrodite.'

'No, Grandmama, I am not. In future I am Charlotte Winterton and will not answer to any other.'

'Our nuptials will not be until May to give us both ample time to get to know each other better and decide if we wish to proceed. I am overjoyed to finally be free of financial worries and be able to think about the future without fear.'

'Persephone, I hope you do not expect me to explain what takes place in the marriage bed.'

'I certainly do not. I can assure you that I know everything necessary.'

Her sister giggled and drew her to one side. 'And are eagerly anticipating your wifely duties as far as I can see.'

'Charlotte! You should not talk of such things. It is unseemly of you.' She tried to sound stern but could not help smiling. 'Ralph intends to bring you out in style; not in London, but at his home. You must promise me you will never say anything so indelicate again.'

'I hope I can say what I want to you, Sister. We are country girls. We might not discuss such immodest matters but we have both seen farmyard animals mating and are well aware of the process.'

Until that moment Seph had managed to keep such images from her head. He was such a very large gentleman and she was a fraction of his size. How the mechanics of such a process took place she was unsure, but one thing she did know: he would never hurt her.

'I think we must not talk about it anymore.' There was a rattle of what sounded like crockery on a tray and they both turned in surprise to see a smartly dressed maid walk in with coffee, chocolate and freshly baked pastries.

Even their grandmother was delighted. 'This is exactly what we wanted. Is the house now fully staffed?'

The girl carefully put the tray down and then curtsied. 'It is, Miss Winterton. Mrs Hopkins has taken charge and has everything organised as it should be.'

After devouring the midday repast they were all feeling much more the thing. 'We must also have a cook — and a very good one if these were anything to go by.' Seph waved the last morsel of her pastry in the air before popping it in her mouth.

'From disaster to delight, Persephone. We were invited reluctantly to spend the festive season with your second cousins. We shall do so much better here where we are welcome guests.'

This was the first positive comment from her relative since they had arrived. 'You shall meet our host, Sir Jeremy, tonight. Dinner will be served in the dining room but you may still have a tray if that is what you would prefer.'

'Absolutely not. I shall retire to my chamber for a rest so that I am fully awake for dinner. Girls, make sure you put on something pretty.'

'If we are to wear an evening gown, Seph, then we must complete our unpacking and see if we can persuade one of the new maids to press them for us.'

With their assistance Grandmama was escorted safely to her own rooms. An elderly maid curtsied on their entrance. 'I am to be your dresser, my lady, whilst you are here.'

This was luxury indeed and Seph and her sister were able to depart knowing they would not be needed.

'Do you think we might have someone to help us, Seph?'

'Shall we find out?'

Indeed, they too now had an abigail. The girl introduced herself as Susan. She had already unpacked all their clothes and sorted out those that needed pressing.

'What shall we do for the remainder of the day? At home we always had tasks to complete as we had no servants to do them for us,' Charlotte said.

'Shall we explore the house that is to be our home for the next two weeks at least? I think I might take you to meet

Sir Jeremy — he is a delightful old gentleman and I think perhaps we do need his permission before we wander about the place as if we are invited guests, not interlopers.'

This time when she knocked on the door she was greeted with a smile by his taciturn retainer. 'Come in, Miss Winterton, Miss Charlotte. The master is receiving in his drawing room.'

Sir Jeremy looked almost animated when they arrived. 'Welcome, welcome, my dears. I am told that the house is now open again.'

They both curtsied politely but he waved them to the seat closest to the fire. 'I am pleased that my home is more welcoming. The storm was serendipitous, do not you think, Miss Winterton?'

'It was indeed, sir. Hopefully, for all of us. There is a blizzard blowing outside so we are unlikely to get any further visitors. When the snow has gone, how soon will the roads be passable again?'

'I fear that the melting snow will only exacerbate the situation. The excess water will add to that already there and it could be several weeks before it is safe for you to travel onwards.'

He looked so delighted at the prospect of them remaining with him she did not have the heart to protest at his forecast. 'We came to ask if we could be allowed to explore your house? We have never set foot in such an impressive building before.'

'You may go where you wish, there are even attics and cellars for you to look inside if you do not object to rodents and spiders.'

'I object to both, Sir Jeremy, so will avoid those places. As we are to be here on Christmas Day, do you have any traditions for this time?'

'I have never decorated the house, and you will be unable to find greenery anyway because of the inclement weather. However, I think we should celebrate in style. There is a family chapel so we can gather there on Christmas morning. I am sure that one of us can say a few appropriate words.

Cook will provide a splendid dinner and we can entertain ourselves with music and charades.'

The thought of Ralph involved in such a pastime made her smile. 'Charlotte can play the piano beautifully and she also has a pretty singing voice.'

'I shall look forward to hearing you perform for us, Miss Charlotte. I do hope Lady Winterton will feel able to join us for dinner today.'

'She has every intention of doing so and is looking forward to meeting you.'

They had been with him for the expected quarter of an hour, so she and her sister stood, politely curtsied, and were shown out. She had yet to see the young girl who had let them in yesterday — no doubt she was busy in the kitchen.

* * *

Ralph was about to enter the stables when someone grabbed his elbow. 'This way, my lord, I need to speak to you away from prying ears.'

The under-coachman pointed to the open door of what looked like a fodder store. Once they were safely inside, and the door closed, his man explained the reason for the secrecy.

'Them two gentlemen have been poking around your carriage, my lord, looking for something. I was able to get close enough to listen. They ain't here to do harm to Sir Jeremy, they're interested in you. I reckon they've been following us since we left London.'

This was extraordinary information. 'Are you sure about this? I have no connection to anyone important. Are they common thieves?'

'I don't reckon so, my lord. They're gentlemen all right, not ordinary folk.'

This was a conundrum that he had to solve. 'Continue to observe and listen and report to me if you discover anything further.'

He returned to the house, puzzled by what he had learned. What could possibly have made those two follow him in such dreadful weather? Then he recalled a strange incident that had occurred outside his club the night before he set out. He had spent an enjoyable evening with friends and on the way home had recalled a debt he had to settle.

Therefore, he had called in briefly at one of his clubs to pay a wager he had lost the previous day. A well-dressed stranger had collided with him and they had both staggered about like a pair of drunken sailors for a few moments.

'I most 'umbly beg your pardon, *je suis désolé, monsieur*, I do not look where I am going. Apologies a thousand times.' The man had untangled himself, raced off and vanished around the corner, pursued seconds later by two men. The man was possibly an aristocratic French émigré.

Ralph had climbed into his vehicle and forgotten about the encounter until today. What had he been wearing that night? He frowned. It had been this very greatcoat; beneath it he had had on his evening rig which he had not worn since. As he had no permanent valet but rather preferred to employ a temporary servant and not take someone around the place with him, these garments were still in his trunk.

He returned to the house the same way he had departed and took the secondary staircase two steps at a time. Once in the privacy of his own apartment, he stripped off his greatcoat and searched all the pockets. There was nothing hidden in any of them.

He tossed the item carelessly onto the nearest chair and headed for the bedchamber. He skidded to a halt on finding Roper busy unpacking his clothes and putting them away. The man was employed as a coachman but was a versatile fellow and had often stepped in and taken the role of manservant when necessary.

'My evening clothes; have you unpacked them as yet?'

'I have indeed, my lord. They are on the rack awaiting the attention of a pressing iron.'

'Did you go through the pockets?'

'I expect you are looking for the letter I found tucked into your waistcoat pocket. I have put it on the side, my lord.'

Ralph nodded and, trying to look nonchalant, collected the square of paper and took it into his sitting room. There was no name or address on the front — nothing to say to whom it was to go to and from whom it came. He snapped the blob of wax and opened it.

The letter was in French. Although he spoke this language well, he was not as proficient at either reading or writing it. He read the sentences in his head and on the third attempt it began to make sense to him.

This was a letter from a French spy with information about the English army and Wellesley's intentions. The two gentlemen were looking for the letter, but were they the intended recipients or English intelligence officers? Until he knew which, he would keep this to himself. The best place to secrete the paper was about his person.

He tucked it into his boot.

'Roper, say nothing of this to anyone, is that clear?'

'Yes, my lord. Do you reckon they're after that letter and have not come here to kill Sir Jeremy?'

'I do. They must not know we have found it.'

'Mum's the word, sir. You can rely on me.'

His man must have guessed that the letter contained secrets of some sort but hopefully wouldn't recall the incident in town that had involved the Frenchman.

If Defoe and Johnson were traitors, they might well be prepared to kill in order to obtain the information within the missive. If they were sent from Horse Guards to recover it, no one was in any danger. How was he to discover this without alerting them?

8

On her return to the drawing room Seph was waylaid by a tall, thin woman dressed in navy blue bombazine. 'Excuse me, Miss Winterton, but Sir Jeremy has said I must come to you for instructions as you are acting as hostess for him.' The woman dipped. 'I am Hopkins, housekeeper here for the moment.'

'Of course, perhaps we could go into the study or library to converse? Charlotte, forgive me, we must do our exploring later.'

Her sister smiled sunnily. 'I shall keep Grandmama company until your return.'

'If you would care to come to my parlour, Miss Winterton, you will find it more convivial than either of those rooms.'

The housekeeper was correct. Despite the fact the room had only been brought back into use in the past hour it was delightfully warm, everywhere spotless, and both tea and coffee waiting for them.

'I see I can leave everything in your capable hands, Hopkins. I assume that Cook will prepare meatless food for Sir Jeremy?'

'The French chef he brought back with him from London last time will continue to take care of his needs. Cook will prepare the meals for everybody else.'

'Will the outside men continue to eat in their own quarters or do they come in now the house is open?'

'They have been taking it in turns to cook, none of them wish to continue if there is an alternative available. If you have no objection, Miss Winterton, they will eat in the servants' hall as they were used to doing.'

'Good. Do you have enough staff to run the house now it is fully opened?'

'I do, thank you.'

The remainder of the conversation was about vegetables, meat and other tedious things. There would be cockerels for Christmas Day itself and she was assured the larder and pantry was well-stocked with anything else that could possibly be needed.

'We will be holding an informal service in the family chapel on Christmas morning and all the staff are welcome to attend if they so wish, but it is not compulsory. Are there any traditions for this household that I should know about?'

'No, Miss Winterton, Sir Jeremy prefers to keep things simple and has never entertained at this time of the year.'

Satisfied Hopkins had everything in hand, Seph hurried back to find her sister so they could resume their exploration of the house. As she approached the drawing room she heard male voices. She increased her pace.

The missing gentlemen were with her sister and grandmother. One would have thought that they were long time acquaintances rather than strangers from the amount of laughter and badinage that was taking place between them.

Charlotte was simpering and fluttering her eyelashes in a way that made her wish to shake her. Why had not their grandmother put a stop to this flirtatious behaviour? She remained in the doorway and cleared her throat noisily. This had the desired effect and all four of them looked towards her.

'Mr Defoe, Mr Johnson, Lord Didsbury has been looking for you. I suggest that you go in search of him yourself as I believe the matter is urgent.' She tapped her foot and stared pointedly at the open doorway. The two gentlemen exchanged glances and for a moment she thought they would remain where they were.

'Then we shall do as you suggest, Miss Winterton.' Defoe, the taller and more personable of the two, said with a charming smile. His companion also stood but he said nothing. She held her breath until they had departed.

'What were you thinking, Sister? You are behaving inappropriately . . . '

Charlotte tossed her head. 'It is not I that was kissing a strange gentleman a few hours ago, so do not poker up at me. I had a chaperone and was doing no more than any other young lady would do when in the company of two delightful gentlemen.'

Seph moved into the room so she could talk to them without fear of being overheard. 'I apologise for being abrupt. You do not understand the situation.' Hastily she explained that Ralph believed the two of them to be not what they appeared.

'Good heavens! We have fallen into a den of thieves and murderers, we would have done better to have remained in the carriage than come here.'

'Grandmama, you are overreacting. We would have frozen to death if we had remained outside. We are perfectly safe here. We have Lord Didsbury, my future husband, to take care of us, remember? In future, could I ask you to be no more than civil to the other gentlemen until we know more about them?'

Her sister agreed a little too readily and this aroused her suspicions. The girl was going to need to be closely supervised until the matter was settled. She could hardly cavil at Charlotte's wild behaviour as hers had been even more reprehensible.

Perhaps there was another way to deal with this volatile situation. 'Remember, my love, that once I am married you will be a substantial heiress. Charming as these two gentlemen are, they are obviously not wealthy or they would not be gallivanting around the countryside without a carriage or change of garments.'

'Mr Johnson explained about that, Seph. However, I do take your point. It would be foolish of me to become entangled with either of these gentlemen when I am sure I shall find myself a baron or maybe even a lord of my own next summer.'

Her grandmother had fallen asleep, a frequent occurrence lately. Her sister immediately spread a comforter across the old lady's knees. Hand in hand they slipped away, leaving her to doze in peace.

* * *

'Lord Didsbury, I believe you wish to speak to us. How can we be of help to you?' Defoe had been lurking in the shadows of the hall and Ralph thought he had deliberately stepped out in order to startle him. Where the hell was the other man?

'Sir Jeremy gave me permission to make free of his house whilst I am here. Would you accompany me to the study where we can talk without fear of being overheard?'

'I should be delighted to, my lord; anything I can do to help.'

There was still no sign of the second man and yet Defoe's previous remark indicated they would both be coming. Ralph had an uncomfortable prickle at the back of his neck and expected at any moment to be struck down from behind.

He was damned if he was going to increase his pace and indicate he was unsettled by having them behind him.

He deliberately slowed down and then stepped aside sharply so they did not cannon into him. As he had suspected, they were both walking directly behind him and because of his manoeuvre were now ahead.

'The library is the next door on the right, gentlemen.'

He had spent some time in the kitchen and had discovered that the chef Sir Jeremy employed was a Frenchman, a genuine émigré, which gave him the perfect opportunity to bring up the subject of possible spies in the household and see their reaction.

They remained standing, which was only correct, and he indicated they should take the two upright chairs in front of the desk. He took the one behind it. Having the substantial width of polished mahogany between him and them was reassuring.

'I need your advice, gentlemen. I was appalled to find that we are harbouring a possible French spy under this roof.'

He kept his expression bland but

watched closely for a reaction. There was none. Johnson nodded. 'Do you mean the chef, my lord? He is what he says he is: a Frenchman who has escaped from the terrors, who does not wish to live under the rule of Bonaparte.'

'We are no more than twenty miles from Dover — do you not find it coincidental that he happens to be working here and not somewhere in London?'

They smiled at each other and then at him in a patronising manner that made him grind his teeth. Somehow he kept his annoyance from showing on his face.

'My lord, he would be more suspicious if he were indeed working in London, where there are vessels in and out of the docks on every high tide. The man does not get more than a half-day off a month. He could not possibly get to Dover and back in that time. Also, on whom would he be spying?'

'A good point, Johnson. Nevertheless, are you aware that he has regular correspondence from London and the mail coach calls no more than two miles from here twice a day?' He had made this up but immediately both men sat straighter and their eyes were sharp. 'Would it not be possible for him to be an intermediary?'

'We did not have that information. You are correct, my lord. That puts a different complexion on the matter.' Defoe and Johnson exchanged glances. Then Defoe continued. 'We must apologise for keeping you in ignorance of our true reason for being here. We are intelligence officers sent from London to recover a letter we think was hidden in your carriage or on your person just before you left.'

Ralph was tempted to reach down and pull out the letter but something stopped him. For some reason, he was not convinced of their *bona fides*. 'I think you are chasing the wrong person for this missing letter. I have had no contact with any Frenchman, apart from the chef when I got here.'

'A man collided with you outside

your club the evening before you set off on your journey and we believe he hid it then.'

'I do recall that incident now that you mention it. You have my permission to search my carriage as long as you do no damage. You must speak to my man, Roper, and he will supervise if you wish to examine the clothes that I was wearing that night.'

'We are dressing for dinner tonight so no doubt your evening clothes will be made ready.'

'I believe that I was wearing them on the night in question and have not had recourse to wear them since. My great-coat is hanging in front of a fire somewhere drying off. There are numerous pockets in that garment so it is possible it is in there somewhere.'

The two exchanged glances and were about to leave when he stopped them. 'I am curious to know, gentlemen, why you have not announced your identity until now. Also, if this letter was hidden somewhere in my carriage or on my person two days ago, how is it that you were able to follow me here?'

Defoe ran his finger around his neckcloth as if it had grown unaccountably tight. 'We were not permitted to identify ourselves. The only way this system works is if we remain anonymous to those we are looking for . . . '

Slowly Ralph pushed himself up so he was looming over them. He was pleased to see they flinched a little in their seats. 'Are you by any chance suggesting that I might be a traitor to this country?' He spoke with icy disdain — every inch the deeply offended aristocrat talking to a lesser mortal.

They both scrambled to their feet. 'No, of course we are not. We apologise if we have caused you any offence by our behaviour. We operate clandestinely; it is in our nature to be secretive even when it would be better to be open.'

He raised an eyebrow. 'That is all very well, but it does not explain how you discovered my identity and were able to follow me.'

Johnson's eyes were hard, his lips almost in a snarl. Then Defoe placed a hand on his companion's arm and the man relaxed a little. Ralph was not entirely convinced by their behaviour that they were indeed what they said they were.

'I have just become betrothed to Miss Winterton. I do not wish this happy occasion to be marred by your ill manners. I hope I make myself perfectly clear.' He nodded and waved a hand in dismissal, then turned his back on them and strolled to the far end of the room as if interested in what was taking place outside.

It was as if there was a target on his back. At any moment he expected Johnson to attack him but instead he heard the door close softly behind the men as they left. Was this the behaviour of villains or frustrated intelligence officers? He was not acquainted with either so had nothing with which to compare.

Only time would tell which they were. In either case, he did not warm to them and intended to ensure they did not spend any time alone with his future wife or her family. He was startled by the sudden banging of a gong which echoed down the passageway.

For a moment he was bemused — did this mean there was a fire? Then he smiled at his error. The noise was to indicate luncheon was being served somewhere. He did not hold with such practices himself and had his staff well-trained so that meals appeared when he wanted them so there was no necessity to bang anything. Also, the fact that he did not entertain meant there were never guests who needed to be reminded.

⋆　⋆　⋆

Seph and Charlotte completed their exploration of the house just as one of the footmen hammered on a large brass gong. 'I am sharp-set, Seph, I do hope that means we are to eat; it seems an age since we broke our fast.'

'I heard a clock somewhere strike midday a while ago so I think you must be right. We had better hurry as Grandmama will wonder at the racket.'

'At least we know where the dining room is. I should hate to be late.'

Ralph was waiting for them in the hall. 'There you are, I have already escorted your venerable relative. Now I shall do the same for you. Our repast is being served in the breakfast room and it is a delicious buffet from which we shall help ourselves.'

'What about the other two guests? Are they to join us?' She looked at him inquiringly.

'I have no idea, but if they wish to eat before dinner then they will have to do so. They are not welcome in the kitchen anymore.'

There was no opportunity to converse privately at present so she would have to follow his lead when dealing with these two gentlemen. Hopefully, they could find an excuse to converse together after luncheon.

Not only were Mr Johnson and Mr Defoe present, but also their host, Sir Jeremy. He was immaculately dressed and looked ten years younger than he had this morning. He and her grandmother appeared to be bosom beaux already.

'If you would care to be seated, I shall serve you.'

She was about to tell him that they were capable of collecting their own food when he winked — a highly risqué action which she hoped no one else had observed.

'Come along, Charlotte, it will be luxury indeed to be served by his lordship.'

'But he doesn't know what we like to eat, Seph,' her sister whispered as she was guided firmly to the table.

'Then we shall tell him politely.'

'That's all very well, but you pushed me past so quickly I have no idea what is on the buffet so how can I tell him what I like?' Her sister's voice had risen so that it was audible to all in the chamber.

He appeared behind them. 'I am all attention. If you would care to be seated then I shall recite to you what is available.'

'This is quite ridiculous, Ralph. It will be far quicker and easier if we help ourselves as everyone else has done.'

She dodged past him to the left and her sister did the same on his right and they were eagerly piling their plates before he had time to intervene. It was a mystery to her why he had wished to act as a footman to them both — there was something she had not grasped about the situation.

The three of them had their backs to the others so it was possible to talk quietly without being overheard. 'Why did you wish us to sit down without you?'

'I thought you might be able to engage the gentlemen in conversation. I have yet to make up my mind about their veracity.'

The conversation around the table was lively; their host was obviously delighted to have company after so long living in isolation. It must be a great relief to him to have Ralph there for his protection.

As she was acting as hostess to this impromptu house party, it was her role to lead the ladies from the room. However, she was not sure how her grandmother would react. The redoubtable old lady might consider her granddaughter was being presumptuous.

Seph placed her napkin and cutlery on her plate and caught her sister's eye. 'Charlotte, if you would assist our grandmother to her feet, we can leave the gentlemen to their conversation.' She had been going to say port, but she was not sure if this was served at any time apart from after dinner. In fact, she rather thought that in the best houses only the ladies ate at midday.

'I should like to return to my room for the remainder of the afternoon, girls, so would you be kind enough to assist me upstairs?'

She exchanged an astonished look with her sister at this remark which was so out of character. They were usually castigated and criticised, but never spoken to so softly.

The two of them left Grandmama to the ministrations of her temporary maid and retreated to the sitting room.

'It is going to be exceedingly difficult to maintain a distance between us all, Seph. When there are so few in a party it is inevitable that we will become closer than would happen in a larger gathering.'

'As long as you are never alone with either of the gentlemen then you can spend as much time as you wish in their company. I am hoping that you will entertain us on the piano in the drawing room after dinner today.'

'I should like that above anything — I must go at once and see if it is in tune, for I refuse to play it otherwise.'

'I shall go to the library to see if I can find myself something more interesting to read than this book of sermons that was all I discovered on the bookshelf.'

9

The library was, as expected, deserted, and no fire had been lit in here so it was unpleasantly cold. Seph's search must be brief. There were no novels of any description, but that was only to be expected in the house of an elderly gentleman who had been a widower for decades. However, there were several interesting books on the flora and fauna of the area and she selected two of those.

She emerged from the chamber, her fingers numb and her toes also. 'There you are, sweetheart, we need to talk and from your demeanour I gather the library is not the place to do it.'

'You're the one who visited the fuel store, Ralph. Is there sufficient there to have the fires lit in all chambers and still be enough to last the winter?'

'I would think there is enough to last

several winters.' He spied a footman carrying cutlery to the dining room and snapped his fingers. 'Make sure the fires are burning everywhere in future.'

'Yes, my lord.' The man attempted to bow and inevitably the silverware slithered from the tray to crash noisily on the boards.

She was about to run to his aid when Ralph grabbed her hand. 'No, he must pick it up himself. It does not do to interfere with a servant's work.'

'Very well, if you insist, but it seems rather unfair to me. What did you wish to speak to me about so urgently?' Her abrupt tone did not please him. She was not going to apologise — if she was to be his wife she must treat him with respect, obviously, but she had no intention of being a subservient spouse. The sooner he knew this, the better their relationship would be in the long-term.

She hurried to warm her freezing fingers at the fire, leaving him to do as he pleased. She stepped back and collided with him. His arms encircled her body, drawing her closer and the contact made her breathless. He rested his chin on the top of her head and sighed theatrically.

'I had no idea I had offered for a shrew, I thought you never spoke a cross word to anyone.'

She relaxed against him and laughed. 'I do not dissemble, I am what you see. I believe that I have an even temper — most of the time. What about you? I am certain with your fiery hair you must have a nature to match.'

His arms tightened and he enveloped her hands within his. 'I am the most peaceable of fellows, positively bovine, I do assure you.'

'Now you are doing it too brown, sir.' She swivelled within his embrace and leaned back against his arms so her weight was entirely supported by him. 'I have not seen you lose your temper. I think that my next task is to provoke you to do so in order that I can see just how formidable you are when enraged.'

There was a glint in his eye that she did not trust. 'I do not recommend that. You might receive in return more than you give.'

'Are you threatening me with physical retaliation? I hardly think that fair, considering the disparity in our sizes.'

'Absolutely not. I believe that if I shout loud enough you will be sufficiently subdued to do as you're told.'

'I shall be deafened but not cowed. I rather think I am going to enjoy getting to know you better.' She moved closer and his grip relaxed. 'I hope if I am fortunate enough to produce children that they have your colouring. I find I am rather partial to red hair.'

The noise he made was more a growl than anything else. The next thing she knew she was being kissed breathless. Her knees were weak and she was obliged to hang onto his coat front in order to remain upright. He removed her hands and turned his back on her in a most impolite fashion. He strode to the far end of the room.

'Remain where you are, I need to be alone.' His voice was barely audible.

She was about to protest but decided to take a seat and wait for him to recover from the experience. 'Are you able to continue a conversation or do you wish me to go completely from the room?' She had the good sense to shout so he could hear her clearly.

He muttered something that she could not catch. 'I think that we must not be alone again, my love, or I shall do something we will both regret.' This time his words were clear.

For a moment she was puzzled, and then understood. 'It was not I that suggested we convene in here unchaperoned. Neither was it I who initiated our embrace. What is it you wish to speak to me about?'

'I have no wish to continue to shout down the room. You are the most provoking young woman.' He turned and strolled back to her, only a slight flush along his cheekbones to indicate he had been at all discommoded by their lovemaking.

He took a seat on the other side of the fire. He then proceeded to explain what he had discovered. 'I would value your opinion; do you think they are genuine and that I should hand them the letter?'

'You must certainly not do that, not at the moment. If they have searched the carriage, and the room, then either they will guess that you are carrying it about your person and attempt to take it by force, or think that they have come on a fool's errand.' He was about to reply when something occurred to her. 'The only way they can know that the Frenchman did not have the letter was if they caught him.'

'God's teeth! You are right. I don't think that it was these two that ran after him. Although I was not paying much attention, I am certain they were older men.'

'Then that is a point in their favour.'

'No, sweetheart, I think it exactly the reverse. Think about it. The French-man was being pursued by the men who wanted to stop him delivering the letter — these must have been the intelligence officers. This means that by the balance of probability, Sir Jeremy is now harbouring traitors under his roof.'

Despite the warmth of the room, a chill ran through her. 'What can we do? We are cut off here and cannot send word to anyone for assistance.'

'Do not look so worried, little one. I guarantee that nothing untoward shall happen to you or your family.'

'That's all very well, Ralph, but I am most concerned for your safety. If they are evil men then they will not hesitate to murder you to get what they want.'

One might have expected him to be suitably shocked by her comment but instead he laughed out loud. This was most vexing and not at all the reaction she had been expecting.

'Darling girl, look at the size of me. Do you really think that even the two of them could overcome me?'

'Your size would be no match for a gunshot.'

'True, but I think it unlikely they will attempt to shoot me or attack me in any way whilst we are still snowed in. There are more than a dozen men here and they would be overwhelmed in no time at all.'

His superior smile did nothing for her temper.

'So, if I am to understand this correctly, my lord, I am to have the pleasure of your company unscathed until the snow melts? At that point they can murder you with impunity and escape.' Her voice was shrill; even to her own ears, she sounded almost hysterical.

Again, he surprised her. In two steps he was at her side, had lifted her from her chair and sat down with her positioned in his lap. He put his arms around her and stroked her back as if she were a child. 'Please, I was teasing. I am in no danger and neither are you. Roper has disabled their pistols — it is I who is armed, not them.'

'But can you be sure they have not discovered the tampering and found replacements?'

'I think it highly unlikely they have done so. Now, shall we talk of something else?'

She smiled and scrambled from his lap. 'If I were to dance with one of them, perhaps I could discover more about their reason for being here?'

'Indeed, you could. You could check to see if he is carrying any further weapons.'

This suggestion was so ludicrous her delightful laughter filled the room. 'And what do you think my grandmother would do if I was to run my hands up and down his person?'

'More to the point, my love, is what I would do if you attempted such a thing. No, do not raise your eyebrows at me, madam. I shall not have it. I should rip the gentleman concerned to pieces with my bare hands.'

'In which case, sir, I shall not attempt such a thing. If we could be serious for a moment, Ralph, I really do not wish to be in close contact with either of them and I do not think that my sister should dance with them.'

'If your sister is playing the piano then she cannot dance with anyone, and I shall stand beside you in a proprietorial manner. I defy the most eager of dancers to approach if I am doing so.'

'Do you play cards?'

'I am famous for my skill. However, I fear you are not talking about games of chance but something tamer.'

'I enjoy playing Whist. Could we not have a hand or two of that? My grandmother is an expert and I expect that Sir Jeremy would be happy to partner her.'

There was a disadvantage to them playing cards without including Defoe or Johnson. This would leave them free to flirt with Charlotte and however determined the young lady was to keep a distance from them, she was not experienced enough to be able to do so without support.

'We need to do something that includes everyone — listening to your sister play must be the entertainment for tonight.'

'Very well, but tomorrow we shall play charades. I shall not take no for an answer.'

He smiled in what he hoped was a non-committal way and she seemed satisfied with this response. He would rather have his teeth pulled than do such a thing and when it came to it, he would find a pressing need to be elsewhere.

★   ★   ★

They spent longer on their preparations than they had ever done before. Having the assistance of a personal dresser seemed to slow things down rather than make them speedier for they each had to wait their turn to be attended to. Eventually Seph and her sister were ready to descend.

'I am so glad that we have evening gowns in the new fashion, Seph, for I expect the gentlemen will dress to impress.'

'There you will be wrong, Charlotte, as Mr Johnson and Mr Defoe do not even have a change of clothes, so they certainly will not have anything for the evening. I expect that Sir Jeremy will be as you say, but I should not be surprised if he wears the old-fashioned breeches and silk stockings.'

They had been talking as if the maid was invisible but she had heard every word and interrupted their conversation. 'Sir Jeremy wears pantaloons and evening slippers, miss. He gave up them other things years ago.'

Seph knew she should dismiss the girl for such impertinence but did not have the heart to do so. Instead she shook her head slightly. 'Susan, I know you have not been trained to hold this position but you should know that a servant never speaks unless spoken to, and certainly does not interrupt the conversation. Please do not do so again.'

The girl curtsied but did not seem at all abashed by the reprimand. 'Begging your pardon, Miss Winterton, I'll remember my place in future. I'm ever so pleased to be here and don't want to lose my position.' She beamed. 'I reckon you both look a treat. It's a shame there's not a grand party tonight for you to show off your lovely gowns.'

It was hard to remain cross when the girl meant no disrespect and was certainly good at her job.

'We shall not be late. You are free until we come up.'

'Lawks, miss, I've got too much to do pressing your other gowns to take time off.'

Ralph must have overheard this conversation as he had wandered into the sitting room to wait for them. He was laughing at the exchange. 'At least the girl is eager to do her job, even if her performance is unusual.'

'We are definitely overdressed for an

informal dinner. You look magnificent in your black, Ralph, but it accentuates your height and bulk. If I did not know you I would be alarmed.'

'And I'm glad that we established our connection before I terrified you by wearing my evening clothes.'

He offered his arm, and she took it, which left her sister to walk alone. Charlotte barely acknowledged his presence and stalked past, gathered up her skirts, and ran lightly down the passageway to vanish before they had scarcely left the room.

'Oh dear! I must be more careful to include my sister. Two days ago we were inseparable and now she is on the outside.'

'I should have thought of that myself. Excuse me, I shall go and apologise. I have no wish to push her into the company of those other two.'

He abandoned her and his long strides took him out of sight in seconds. She was only halfway to the gallery when she heard the other gentlemen emerging from their apartment ahead. Instinctively she increased her pace and was almost running by the time she reached the corner.

Her smile was rueful. If they had observed her ridiculous behaviour they would think her to be hurrying after Ralph. Her hands clenched. Was it possible they would interpret her actions correctly? Had she inadvertently revealed she knew they were not who they purported to be?

After several steadying breaths she was ready to put right the possible damage she had done. There was no sign of her sister or her betrothed. She sighed loudly, knowing they would hear her. Then she turned to speak to them.

'I am so put out. Lord Didsbury abandoned me to walk on my own and went after my sister. Perhaps one of you would do me the courtesy of accompanying me to dinner in his stead?'

She had addressed her remark to Mr Johnson who was closest to her. His smile appeared genuine. 'I should be delighted to, Miss Winterton. I hope there is not trouble so soon in your relationship.'

'Oh no, nothing like that, I do assure you. He was right to find Charlotte and apologise as we had upset her. However, he should not have left me to walk by myself. I could have gone with him.'

'Might I be permitted to say that you look delightful this evening? That gown complements your colouring to perfection.'

Her hand was now resting on Johnson's arm and she detected tension in it. 'If I am not mistaken, sir, although you are not in evening clothes, you are certainly wearing something different from before. How is that possible?' No sooner had she asked the question than she regretted her words. She should have responded prettily to his compliment.

'You are most observant, Seph. Sir Jeremy has kindly supplied us with what we need until our carriage can return with our trunks. These garments are decidedly old-fashioned as they were worn by him in his youth.'

'Our host must have been much taller then. My grandmother insisted that she was almost as tall as me when my age which I find hard to believe.'

Defoe was walking slightly behind them and now joined in the conversation. The arm she was holding was no longer rigid. This was a good thing.

'What is fortunate, Miss Winterton, is that my friend and I are roughly the same build. We are going to look sadly underdressed this evening, I fear.'

'You will be bright birds amongst two crows, sir, so must not be bothered about such things.' She smiled in what she hoped was a convincing way. 'I must say, gentlemen, that I have always admired brightly coloured waistcoats and silver threads in a jacket.'

They both laughed which was the outcome she had aimed for and she was sanguine that if there had been a danger of alerting them, it was now averted.

She had forgotten the light-hearted conversation she had had with Ralph about her spending time with these gentlemen. The three of them were exchanging badinage, laughing gaily as they walked down the stairs together.

Something made her look up and he was standing in the centre of the hall, watching them closely. His expression was bland, but she already knew him well enough to know he was displeased. Whether it was with her or them, she would no doubt discover sometime in the future.

'Ralph, see how smart these gentlemen are, thanks to the good offices of Sir Jeremy.'

He nodded and walked towards them. He was surprisingly light on his feet for such a big man. 'Thank you for escorting my future wife, gentlemen, but I shall take her now.'

This casual reference that made her sound like a parcel, rather than a person, was enough to annoy her. 'I am content where I am. Is Lady Winterton down?'

His eyes narrowed but he could hardly snatch her away. 'She is enjoying a comfortable coze with Sir Jeremy. Charlotte has forgiven us and is searching for suitable music to play later.'

As soon as they were in the drawing room she removed her hand from Mr Johnson's arm and smiled her thanks for his escort.

'There you are at last, Persephone. I have told you a dozen times that being tardy is unacceptable.' Her grandmother was assisted to her feet by their host. 'If dinner has been ruined, then it is you we shall blame.'

She was used to being unfairly called to account and ignored it but Ralph would not let it go. 'Lady Winterton, if anyone is to blame then it should be Mr Defoe, as he was in fact three steps behind Mr Johnson and your granddaughter. Therefore, your opprobrium should be centred on him, do not you think?'

'That's as may be, my lord. The other two are no concern of mine. The fact that they are late as well does not excuse my granddaughter.'

Their host caught her eye, smiled but said nothing to exacerbate the situation. He was really a charming old gentleman. The fact that they had all turned up on his doorstep so unexpectedly was not only of benefit to her and her family, but also to him.

Dinner consisted of two courses; each with several removes and quite delicious. The conversation flowed and even her grandmother became less curmudgeonly after two glasses of excellent claret. Neither she nor her sister touched alcohol but she could not help but be aware that the three younger gentlemen drank deeply.

At the end of the meal, the ladies left them to the port. Charlotte — she could even think of her sister by that name now — took her arm and drew her aside. 'Did you see how much they consumed? It was as if they were having a competition to see who could drink the most alcohol. They will all be in their cups and I have no wish to remain here if that is so.'

'And nor do I. Grandmama is almost asleep. Shall we take her up before they join us? I have no wish to be here if it comes to fisticuffs.'

For once there was no opposition to their suggestion that their ancient relative should retire at once. She was left in the capable hands of her abigail, who appeared to know her place better than the girl they had.

'Shall we retire or do you wish to go downstairs again, Seph?'

'Stay up here, it will be safer and quieter. I can hear raised voices coming from the dining room. I feel sorry for Sir Jeremy but I am sure Ralph will keep him safe.'

10

Ralph's ploy to get the two possible villains drunk failed miserably. Sir Jeremy fell face-first onto the table before that happened, and he was obliged to carry the unfortunate old gentleman back to his apartment. When he returned, Defoe and Johnson were no longer there, and neither were the ladies.

His capacity to consume alcoholic beverages without showing any adverse effect was legendary. One of the few advantages of being so massive, he suspected. He had taken it upon himself to act as the owner of this establishment as Sir Jeremy seemed oblivious to the rest of the house.

The doors were bolted, even the side door, and the windows and shutters safely latched. Was he locking in the danger rather than keeping it out? Where the hell had the other two gone?

He took the stairs two at a time. There was a light flickering under the door of the girls' sitting room so they were obviously still up. He stopped outside the apartment that Defoe and Johnson were occupying and could see a similar glow from there. Satisfied, he decided he might as well retire early himself.

Having the letter beneath his foot in his evening slipper had been uncomfortable, but at least he had known it was safe there. When he removed it, he pushed it into the toe of his boot where it would now remain until the morning.

As he settled into bed he tried to recall how long there was until Christmas Day. So much had happened in the three days they had been here that he had lost track of time. The household would continue as usual, making some allowances for the festive season, and for that he was profoundly grateful. He did not hold with the nonsense that often took place at this time of year.

Putting his face into a pile of flour in order to remove a live bullet or, even worse, risking being severely burnt in order to pull a raisin from a bowl of burning alcohol was not his idea of sensible behaviour. The thought that he might be forced to join in such things filled him with horror. He was smiling when he fell asleep.

The next day passed with no incidents of note and he was no closer to discovering the true identity of the other guests. They did not come down for breakfast and he had to assume they had consumed so much wine they were suffering the after-effects.

'Seph, is it Christmas Day tomorrow or the day after?'

'Tomorrow is Christmas Eve, Ralph, I cannot believe you have forgotten the date.'

'I was thinking that you might be expecting a gift of some sort. That the staff must be given something on Boxing Day.'

'Sir Jeremy must take care of the latter. I think it strange that he has handed over the running of the house to us. I hope he does not expect that we shall remain here when the weather improves.'

'And a gift? You have not answered my question.'

'I expect neither to give nor receive presents this year. Next year, when we are married, things will be different. Are you any nearer to deciding exactly who those gentlemen really are?'

'I think we shall not know the truth until it is possible to leave here. But my feeling is that they are traitors, not intelligence officers as they claim.'

'That is my opinion too. Susan, the maid who is taking care of us, is adamant that the floods will recede a week after the snow melts.'

'If that's true, then there is no prospect of leaving for at least two weeks.'

'You do not seem especially gloomy at the prospect, Ralph. I for one, shall be relieved to be away from here. I am not sleeping well and am constantly waking thinking that at any moment you might be attacked by those two men.'

'Would you be happier if I arranged for Roper to sleep in my dressing room?'

Her smile was radiant and not for the first time he wondered how he had ever thought her plain. 'Yes, that would be wonderful. Do you not think it is astonishing how involved we are when less than a week ago we did not know of each other's existence?'

'Fate, or a higher hand, brought us together. I shudder to think to whom I might have eventually been married if I had not met you.'

'To be honest, I had no thought of being married to anyone. I was hopeful that my sister might find herself a husband but I was resigned to being a spinster.'

He wanted to snatch her up and show her just how wrong she was but thought if they were not to pre-empt their wedding vows he had better keep his distance.

Her eyes widened and he knew she had understood how much he wanted to make love to her.

'It is going to be increasingly difficult for me to stay away from you, darling. Can I not persuade you to bring the wedding forward? We could call the banns as soon as we are at Didsbury.'

'Ask me that when we are able to leave. I shall know you better then. Although our acquaintance will be short, we shall have spent more time together than most betrothed couples do in six months.'

★   ★   ★

When he looked at her so intensely, he was hard to resist. She had not thought herself a sensual woman, had scarcely noticed any other gentleman however handsome they might have been, yet there was something about this big bear of a man that touched her heart, and other parts of her anatomy that must not even be thought about.

With ingenuity and determination, they were managing to avoid being alone but also to spend a satisfying amount of time together. The day had sped past and the snow had stopped at last but it showed no sign of thawing. It would be Christmas Eve tomorrow and yet the house and its occupants continued about their daily tasks as if the Lord's birthday was not rapidly approaching.

Even in their straitened circumstances they always exchanged a gift on the day itself. 'Charlotte, I think it might be best to keep the small items we have made for each other in their hiding places until we are elsewhere.'

'I thought that too. There is a strange feel in this house, it is as if we are cut off from the rest of the world . . . '

'Hardly surprising, dearest, as we are exactly that.'

Her sister laughed. 'You know what I meant so please do not pretend you do not understand. There is no sign that it is the festive season, not even a single branch of greenery, an extra candle or even the smell of a figgy pudding steaming in the kitchen. It could be any other time of the year.'

'We shall have an informal prayer meeting in the chapel to mark the day. There will be a special dinner, so Hopkins told me, and on Boxing Day we will have a cold collation and the staff have the day off.'

'As long as we do not have to wait on them, I am content to look after ourselves. After all, it is what we are more accustomed to doing, is it not?'

Dinner that night was equally delicious. The two gentlemen again drank themselves into a stupor but Sir Jeremy and Ralph were more abstemious. For a second night in a row their grandmother had to be assisted to bed and they retired early.

* * *

She was woken by her sister shaking her shoulder. 'You will not believe it, Seph. The snow has all but gone. I thought I heard it raining in the night and I was correct. We shall be able to leave here in a few days and return to civilisation.'

'I think our stay here has been very civilised, Sister, certainly a lot more convivial than it would have been if we were where we were supposed to be, at our cousin's house. There we are treated as poor relations . . .'

'Which we are, so we cannot blame them for that.' Charlotte rushed into the dressing room and began her morning ablutions.

'What time is it? I must have overslept for I never awake after you.'

'It is a little after nine o'clock so we are both tardy.'

Seph went to see this remarkable change in the weather for herself. Her sister had been right, the snow had miraculously vanished, leaving a soggy park and grey sky. 'If it has rained again then the floods will be far worse than they were before. Also there has just been a mountain of snow melt into them. Susan said it will be at least a week after the snow has gone before we can attempt to depart.'

Naturally she had raised her voice as her sister was now splashing about in the dressing room and she was standing by the window.

'I'm sure that you are correct, but might I ask you to not yell like a fishwife. It is most unbecoming of you.'

Ralph's voice came from the other side of the wall. He was in their sitting room where he had no right to be. Quite forgetting she was wearing only her nightgown she rushed to the door to remonstrate with him.

At her sudden appearance his expression changed from amused to something else entirely. 'I beg your pardon, I had forgotten — pray excuse me.' She retreated and slammed the door, causing her sister to step out of the dressing room with no clothes on at all.

'He is in the sitting room and I went out like this.'

Her sister hastily stepped out of sight before answering. 'He has no right to be lurking about in there without our permission. It is a good thing you are engaged to be married is all I can say on the matter.'

'This would not have happened if Susan had come as she should with our morning chocolate at seven o'clock. I wonder what has kept her from us.'

Again, he spoke from the other room. 'Forgive me for eavesdropping, but your missing maid is the reason I intruded. She has vanished from the premises and despite a thorough search we have yet to locate her.'

Seph snatched up her bedrobe, pulled it on and joined him. 'The snow has gone, is it possible she decided to return home for some reason?'

'She shares an attic room with one of the kitchen maids and she was missing when the girl woke. It appears she did not sleep in her bed last night.'

'I dismissed her at nine o'clock and she said she was going straight to her room.' Then a dreadful thought occurred to her. 'Have you searched all the bedchambers?'

He understood immediately to what she was referring. He changed in an instant from a man she knew and was slowly falling in love with, to a formidable stranger.

'I fear you might be right.' He said no more but turned and she heard him hammering on the door further down the corridor.

She was dressed and ready in record time, as was her sister, who had overheard this conversation but didn't understand the significance.

'Why should she be in there with them? Surely they would prefer one of the footmen to assist them?'

'She will not have gone there willingly and they might well have done her serious hurt.'

Her sister was remarkably innocent for a girl of seventeen years and she had no intention of enlightening her at this moment. Seph vividly recalled an incident that had taken place in their home village two years ago. A young girl had been brutally attacked by a young gentleman — if he could be called such after what he did — who was visiting the area. He had violated her and if the villagers had managed to lay their hands on him he would not have survived the experience. The young girl certainly did not, as when she discovered she was with child, she took her own life.

Susan could not be more than fifteen years of age, little more than a child. She sent up a fervent prayer to the Almighty that she was wrong in her assumptions and there was an innocent explanation for the girl's absence.

The corridor was eerily silent when she emerged. No raised voices, no signs of violence and she was sure there would be if Ralph had discovered the girl violated in one of their beds. If Susan was not there then why had he not come out? Why could she not hear him talking to them?

She hovered outside the door he had gone through and was just raising her hand to knock when it flew open and he emerged. From his expression he had found nothing untoward in there.

He grabbed her arm and moved her rapidly back into her home domain before he spoke. 'She was not there and they are both comatose from the amount of alcohol they consumed. There was an empty decanter on the sideboard so I think they must have taken the brandy up with them when they retired.'

'I am relieved Susan was not there but am now very concerned for her safety. Where else could she be if she did not go out? Were all the doors still bolted?'

'They were, which is why I know she is still somewhere in the house.'

'Charlotte and I are ready to help with the search. Have you involved the other servants? They have all worked here for many years and know the house better than we do.'

'Unfortunately, Susan isn't one of them. She was visiting with Hopkins, she is her great-niece, and was happy to be offered employment. And in answer to your question, Roper is organising those not needed to look everywhere systematically.'

'There is a staircase at the far end of this passageway that leads directly to the attics. I have seen Susan go through it. Shall we start there?'

When she went to push the door it refused to budge. There was something behind it. Her stomach lurched. She looked at him and his concern was obvious.

'Leave it to me, Seph, I'll find another way down and bring her out. I hope to God she is merely unconscious and has not broken her neck. Try calling to her, she might rouse at the sound of your voice.'

Despite doing as he said there was an ominous silence from behind the door. A short while later she heard voices approaching down the stairs.

'Susan, lie still whilst I check you have no broken bones. Does your head hurt very much?'

She pressed her ear to the door in the hope of hearing a response but could hear nothing through the wood. Ralph spoke again. 'You have taken a nasty tumble; you have nothing broken but a severe head wound and have lost a lot of blood. You will need sutures in the gash.'

'I have the necessary items in my travelling bag, my lord, if you can bring her out this way then she can go in our bed where we can take care of her.'

There was some thumping and shuffling and then the door was pulled open and he stepped out, the girl limp and white in his arms.

'She is still alive, but barely.'

Roper appeared behind his master. 'Fetch me boiled water, clean cloths and a jug of warm, sweetened half wine, half water. Be as quick as you can, her life depends on it.'

The girl was too cold, too pale, and she feared there would not be a happy outcome to this incident. She and her sister stripped the patient and put her in one of their own nightgowns and then wrapped her in a warm comforter and put her under the covers.

'Make the fire up, Charlotte, we need to get the room as warm as possible. When you have done that can you rush to the kitchen and ask for hot bricks wrapped in red flannel to be fetched up here?'

'Will she die? I wish we had found her sooner.'

'We must pray for a Christmas miracle, for nothing else will save her. She had been there too long.'

Seph did her best, cleaned the wound and stitched it up then placed a clean bandage around, holding the dressing in place. Then began the arduous task of trickling the watered wine into the girl's mouth in the hope that it would replace the lost blood.

The hot bricks arrived and were placed around the unconscious girl. There was nothing more she could do so she stepped away, shocked to find her gown quite ruined.

Ralph had been there all this time and she had not realised; his shirt and waistcoat were in little better shape than her dress. 'I have done all I can, even a physician could not have done any more. My sister can continue to spoon liquid into her whilst I change. I think you had better do the same, my dear.'

He opened his arms and without hesitation she walked into his embrace. She leaned against him, his warmth and strength a comfort to her. 'It is Christmas Eve, if there is going to be a miracle today seems the ideal time. She is young and strong and there is still hope whilst she breathes.'

'I feel so awful I did not hear her fall. She had been there for twelve hours and not come around. This is a very bad sign, very bad indeed. I think that her great-aunt should be with her. Would you be so kind as to fetch her?'

'Do I have time to change or do you think I should bring her here immediately?'

She looked at the scarcely breathing shape beneath the covers. 'I think now would be best.'

11

Ralph found the housekeeper waiting at the bottom of the main staircase. 'Miss Winterton suggests that you go to the sickroom immediately.'

There was no need to tell her anything else; she gathered her skirts and raced past him.

There was a sombre atmosphere as if somehow the accident had cast a pall over the place. This was supposed to be the most joyous time of the year, the time that Christians everywhere celebrated the arrival of the Christ Child. Now he feared they would be mourning the loss of the maid.

It was doubtful that Sir Jeremy was aware of the accident. It had happened under his roof and the staff were ostensibly employed by him, so he should be informed immediately. When he knocked on the door he was admitted at once.

'The master had been expecting you to come, my lord. He is most anxious to hear about the little lass.'

How the hell did the news travel here so fast? 'Who informed him?'

'Molly, the girl you met the night you arrived; she is our eyes and ears here.'

Ralph briefly explained what had transpired to his host. The gentleman shook his head and wiped his eyes with a voluminous silk handkerchief.

'How shocking, how dreadful, her great-aunt must be beside herself.'

'Hopkins is sitting with her great-niece. She will remain there until things improve or they do not.'

'The snow has gone; you will be able to leave here by the start of the year if there is no further rain.'

'I shall send one of my men out to investigate the state of the road and surrounding countryside. As soon as it is clear he will take your letter and mine to my lawyers. I gave my word I would get your will ratified before I depart and

I do not break a promise.'

'I was hoping you might invite me to accompany you to your own house, sir. I am loath to part with the Wintertons or yourself.'

'I should be delighted to have you come. After all, you took us in and have made us very welcome. I shall pay the wages of the staff you have employed to take care of us so that they can remain here until the summer. Miss Winterton and I will be married in May and no doubt my bride will wish to take a wedding trip somewhere.'

'I understand exactly. If I can remain until your nuptials that would be more than I expected. Then Lady Winterton and Miss Charlotte can return here with me and remain until you are in residence at your own place once more.'

'That sounds an excellent solution, sir. I shall get your coachmen to prepare your carriage so it is ready to move when we are.' He nodded politely. 'I hope you will excuse me, I must return to the sickroom and see how things go. You will be informed of any changes.'

They both knew what he actually meant was that when the girl went to meet her maker, he would send word. He didn't knock but walked straight in. 'Is there any change?' He directed his question to Seph, who was standing by the window.

'She is no worse, but no better either. If only we could get her warm I think she would have a slight chance of mending. In my experience a patient that remains unconscious for so long is more likely to die than recover.'

They both turned when there was a knock on the sitting room door. 'I'll see who that is. Stay here, sweetheart and do what you can.'

Johnson, looking grey and poorly, was leaning against the doorjamb. 'I heard about the girl. We should have heard her fall as our bedchamber is the nearest to the staircase. If we had not been so damned drunk we might have been able to help.'

He looked so wretched that Ralph began to revise his opinion of this gentleman. Perhaps he was indeed an intelligence officer and not the villain he thought him.

'It was an accident, nobody's fault. The next few hours will decide the outcome. There is something you could do to help now, if you and your companion are well enough.'

The man straightened and looked a little less miserable. 'Anything, just ask, my lord.'

'Two things — the first is to inform Sir Jeremy's coachmen that he will be needing his carriage as soon as the weather clears, as he's going to accompany the Wintertons and myself to Didsbury. The second — to ride to the road and see if the floods have receded sufficiently for anything to get through.'

'We will see to it at once.' He pushed himself upright. 'I give you my word, sir, that from now on we will consume less alcohol and behave better. Sir

Jeremy does not deserve for us to take such advantage of his hospitality.'

He offered his hand and it was shaken vigorously. There was no sign of Defoe. 'Is your companion still feeling the after-effects of his overindulgence?'

'No — or rather yes, he is not in his bed but has gone for some fresh air in the hope that this will clear his head. I shall find my coat and join him so we can complete your tasks.'

The door was closed softly, showing respect for the patient.

'I'm beginning to believe we were wrong about those two, but I shall bide my time before taking the next step.' He did not mention the letter secreted in his boot but she understood at once to what he was referring.

'I think that you are correct to be cautious. This is not an auspicious start to Christmas.'

'As we were not intending to celebrate, merely to attend a prayer meeting tomorrow morning, I hardly think it makes any difference to our plans.'

Her smile was sad. 'A week ago, we were closing down the house and preparing to travel to our cousin's house for an extended stay. Now I am watching at the bedside of a dying girl. I am betrothed to you and acting as hostess for Sir Jeremy and I did not know either of you until a few days ago. The fact that there are possibly two dangerous villains in our midst is even more extraordinary.'

'I am equally bemused at how my life has changed. I'm not known for being impulsive; I rarely make a decision without giving it serious thought. You are the best thing that has ever happened to me, I hope one day you will feel the same about me.' He had not meant to say this but it was too late to repine.

She closed the gap between them and placed one hand on his chest. It took all his willpower not to take her in his arms. 'You are still prepared to marry me knowing that I do not feel as strongly as you?'

'I would marry you even if I knew that you disliked me profoundly. I am arrogant enough to believe I shall change your mind over time.'

'I am very fond of you, I admire you, I respect you and I most definitely find you desirable. I believe that will be enough to make ours a happy union. I am hopeful we will have children of our own and this will bring us closer.'

The thought was almost too much for his control. Gently he removed her hand and put a safe distance between them. 'If Hopkins is to remain here with her niece, who will take over her responsibilities?'

'I shall speak to Cook. This is not a large household and I think it will run smoothly without a housekeeper at least for a day or two.'

★　★　★

Charlotte would take care of their grandmother and make sure she was fully informed of the circumstances. It occurred to Seph that she would have to make fresh arrangements for herself and her sister, as they could not use their own bedchamber. If the girl died then she was not sure she would wish to return to that bed.

She shook her head and frowned at such a selfish thought. There were no more guest rooms in this section of the dwelling. They would have to sleep in the main part of the house, but before she set things in motion she must speak to Sir Jeremy and ensure he had no objection to them using these private rooms.

Everyone was subdued, the house unnaturally quiet, and even the footmen were creeping about as if the death had already taken place. Her host was happy for her and Charlotte to move into a different apartment.

'Such a tragedy, to lose your life so young.'

'Susan is still alive, Sir Jeremy, and we must pray that she makes a full recovery. However, I am not confident this will be the case. Thank you for allowing us to use your family rooms. I have suggested that there is no formal dinner tonight. There will be a cold collation set out and we shall help ourselves when we wish to.'

'Exactly so. No one is in the mood for anything else. Is Lady Winterton receiving this morning?'

'I believe so, she is remaining in her apartment but I am sure will welcome a visit from yourself.'

Seph had eaten nothing so far today and had asked for coffee and whatever was available to be served in the drawing room, where she found Ralph.

'I am glad that you have come, as I have information for you. The water is receding more quickly than any of the locals expected. The road should be passable in two or three days, not two weeks as we were told.'

'What have you decided to do?'

He looked around to ensure there was no one lurking in the shadows who could overhear him. 'I have decided to take the letter to Horse Guards myself. This solves the problem, don't you think?'

'I think it an excellent idea. If they are *bone fide* they will not care when the letter is returned as long as it does not fall into the wrong hands.' She stopped as something less pleasant occurred to her. He was before her.

'And if they are not, then the matter is of some urgency to them and they will attempt to force me to give it up before we leave.'

He seemed remarkably cheerful about the prospect of being violently attacked. He must think himself invincible. 'Ralph, it will be impossible to relax until we are away from here. I hope you are keeping Roper close by. That you have warned the other footmen to be on their guard?'

'I can hardly do that as they are not privy to the secret. Here, my dear, have your coffee and pastry and we shall talk of something more cheerful.'

There was nothing convivial she could think of so they remained in companionable silence. When she had done she replaced her used crockery on the sideboard. 'I am going upstairs to see how Susan does.'

He followed her and she was glad to have his support. No one had come to her to say there had been a change in the girl's condition but at least there had been no message saying she had died.

There was the soft murmur of voices coming from the bedroom that had been hers and she burst into the room, not believing what she saw. Susan was sitting up, drinking from the silver beaker that she was holding herself.

'I cannot tell you how glad I am to see you awake. When did this happen?' She addressed her remark to the house-keeper.

'No more than a quarter of an hour ago, Miss Winterton. I was about to send word to you.'

Seph hurried across and felt the girl's pulse. It was strong and steady, her colour was good and there was no fresh blood on the bandage round her head. This was nothing short of a Christmas miracle.

Hawkins smiled benevolently. 'She has

had three full beakers of watered wine and is asking for something to eat.'

'Susan, do you feel at all nauseous? Are you dizzy? Do you have the headache?'

The girl giggled. 'My head is spinning, but I reckon it's the wine. It hurts a bit, but nothing too bad. I'm ever so sorry I've caused all this upset, Miss Winterton. I put my foot through my skirt and went flying backwards. I should have been more careful.'

'You were deeply unconscious for a long time so you must remain where you are for at least another day.'

'I was going to move her to my room, miss. She can hardly stay where she is, it would not be proper.'

'Miss Charlotte and I are moving so Susan can stay here for the present. Perhaps you would like to share the bedchamber whilst she is here, Hawkins?'

'I shall send another girl to move your belongings, Miss Winterton. I must get back to my duties . . . '

'There is no need, everything is in hand. You will be doing me a favour if you remain to take care of your great-niece.'

The matter settled to everyone's satisfaction, she retreated to find Ralph lounging on the window seat. 'I am overjoyed that the girl is going to make a full recovery. I am as surprised as you that she has done so.'

She held out her hand and after a moment's pause he surged to his feet and took it. 'Come with me to inspect the family chambers. I need to know where my sister and I will be sleeping for at least the next two or three nights.'

All the rooms they looked at were neglected, unlike the remainder of the house which had been maintained to a high standard. 'You cannot use any of these; they are damp and vermin-infested. I doubt they have been used for decades.'

'I can hardly go back on my word and insist that the girl moves back to her attic.'

He looked at her as if she was speaking in tongues. 'She is a servant, not a member of your family; she will do as she is bid. You will be running my household soon enough and must learn to keep your staff at a distance. It does not pay to fraternise.'

This was a side to him she did not know and did not much care for. 'I disagree. As far as I'm concerned, I am fortunate not to be in the same situation as they are. I intend to treat staff as valued employees, show them the respect they deserve . . . '

'That is nonsense, and you would soon be in an invidious position if you behaved like that. Good God, you sound like a revolutionary.'

'And you sound like a gentleman I cannot like. I suggest that you take yourself elsewhere and leave me to organise my own life as I have been doing these past five years.'

He stepped back as shocked as if she had slapped him hard across the face. She doubted he had ever been spoken to like this and for a moment regretted her outburst. Then she straightened her spine and gave him stare for stare.

He muttered something that made her ears burn and strode out of the room. From the noise he made, he was taking the stairs at least two at a time. He was not at all pleased with her.

Seph thought it wise to allow him to recover his temper before she apologised for her shrewish remark. He was right to point out that their lives had been completely different up until this point. Indeed, the more she thought about it, the less she wanted to make the arrangement permanent. Wishing to share your bed with a gentleman was not the same as wishing to share the rest of your life.

Should she break off the engagement immediately or allow her family to live in luxury for a few weeks before they were obliged to return to the penury of their own existence? This would be an extremely duplicitous action on her part and very unfair to Ralph, but it was always possible she might change her mind when she got to know him better. He was a forceful aristocrat, used to having his own way in all things. She was not sure she was prepared to give up her independence and become what was, in law, his possession.

Good heavens! Young ladies married gentlemen for status, wealth and prosperity or for their families all the time without having the connection that she already had with Ralph. To even contemplate cancelling the betrothal would be the height of folly. To do so would be selfish and stupid.

The matter settled to her satisfaction in her head, she went to speak to Hawkins in the hope she might be able to suggest a suitable bedchamber. When she arrived, it was to find two girls busily changing the linen on the bed and no sign of its previous occupant.

'Susan's feeling ever so much better, Miss Winterton, and has gone back to her own room so you can remain here.'

The first thing to do was find her

sister and give her the good news. After looking in Grandmama's room with no luck she tried all the reception rooms and even the kitchen. Where on earth had her sister vanished to? Surely, she had not gone outside?

Then her sister ran up to her. 'You will not credit what I've just heard. There are secret passages in this house. There is one in the drawing room. Will you search for it with me?'

'I have nothing more interesting to do so I should be thrilled to help, as long as I am not required to enter it myself.'

Charlotte ran across to the fireplace and began to press and twiddle the carved flowers that surrounded it. To her astonishment, there was a grating sound and the wall opened up in front of them.

'How exciting! Wait a minute; we must find candles and then we can explore together.' Seph peered into the gloom and the cobwebs and decided she would not allow her sister to go in.

How had Charlotte known where to press?

'I do not think we should go in without telling someone, Charlotte.' These were wasted words as her sibling had already vanished through the opening in the panelling. She had no option but to grab a lit candle and follow her.

As soon as she stepped inside the narrow passage, the door mysteriously closed behind her. Presumably it was set to do so, but she would have preferred to have had it left open. Her heart thudded painfully and she was finding it hard to breathe.

'Charlotte, how did you discover this?'

'The girl who works for Sir Jeremy showed me. I have no idea how she knew. If we go to the end of this bit and then turn right it leads to a flight of steps and then we will emerge near the stables. If we go the other way, we will end up in Sir Jeremy's domain.'

'We are not dressed for this, sweetheart. We must find something warmer before we go any further.'

They returned to the entrance but despite running her fingers over the entire panel, tapping and pushing, it remained firmly closed. 'We will have to call out. Someone will hear us eventually and we can explain to whomever it is how the door opens from their side.'

After banging and shouting for a considerable time, Seph realised no one was going to come to their rescue. 'I cannot understand why no one has heard us.'

'I am not interested in anything apart from the fact that my candle is about to burn out and I'm getting very cold,' Charlotte said.

'Then we have no option but to find our way to the stables whilst we still have the light from mine. We cannot be any colder than we are already, and it will take us but minutes to make our way from the exit to the warmth of the house.'

The passage was longer than she had expected but eventually they came to the steps which were slippery and dangerous. Being so cold and concerned for her sister's well-being had made her aversion to darkness and spiders less urgent. The walls were also slimy with some sort of vegetation and she was relieved when they reached the bottom without either of them twisting their ankle.

'What if the door is locked from the outside? What if we can't get out? Your candle is almost finished and I refuse to go back down these passageways in complete darkness.'

'Charlotte, this was your idea so you must remain brave until we are safe again.'

Fortunately, the door moved when she pushed it and with a sigh of relief she took her sister's hand and led her through. She was about to express her delight at having found their way out when someone put a sack over her head, followed by a rope holding her upper limbs fast to her side.

She could scarcely breathe. The noxious material filled her mouth and nostrils when she tried to scream. Her heart was banging so loudly she could hear it in her ears. Her sister would be terrified.

Her sister had been duped. The girl must be working for those men who had finally revealed their true natures. They were indeed the traitors Ralph had thought them to be all along. Having failed to find the letter they were resorting to violent means in order to persuade him to give it up.

Charlotte was not a strong girl, emotionally or physically, and might never recover from the experience of being abducted and manhandled. She was made of sterner stuff and was sure she was resilient enough to withstand whatever was coming next. The men would not harm them: they might be the worst kind of villains, but they were not stupid. They would never leave here alive if either she or her sister were injured in any way.

She braced herself as one of the two picked her up as if she were a sack of coal and slung her over their shoulder. She feared she would empty her bladder and if she did it would serve him right. The journey was mercifully short and before she disgraced herself she was tossed roughly into a room of some sort and the door was slammed shut.

With some difficulty she steadied her breathing, and managed to calm herself sufficiently to attempt to speak even though hooded by a stinking sack. 'Charlotte, are you all right?'

There was no answer. Was her sister unconscious? She held her breath so she could hear any sounds. There were none. She was alone in this prison — they had taken her sister elsewhere.

12

Ralph's anger had gone before he reached the hall but he was damned if he was going to go back and continue the conversation. He could hardly expect her to understand how things were done when they had been living like church mice for the past few years. She was an intelligent woman and would soon see for herself that making friends of the servants was something they did not expect and would not like.

He treated his employees properly, paid them fairly and expected to be well-served in return. He even provided them with a pension and a cottage when they were too old to continue working. The world was not equal: everyone had their place, and the sooner she understood that the happier she would be in her new position as his wife.

Roper appeared with his outdoor garments — the man was proving to be an excellent valet and he thought he would make this a permanent position. 'You need to dispense with that livery, you are my manservant now.'

'Yes, my lord. I thank you for your confidence in my abilities to take care of you. Am I not to drive your coach any longer?'

'That is up to you. As my man you will accompany me everywhere and if you wish to continue to act as coachman as well then I am happy with that.'

Ralph shrugged into his caped riding coat, tied his muffler around his neck and rammed his hands into his leather gloves. He disdained the use of head-gear and rarely wore a beaver like other gentlemen.

He was halfway to the stables when he thought he should have told Roper of his decision with regard to the letter. He would do so when he returned. Although his breath steamed in front of him, he doubted the temperature was much below freezing. It would actually be beneficial if the weather remained icy as the roads would be easier to negotiate if they were not axle-deep in sticky mud.

His beloved made no attempt to seek him out and he decided it might be advisable to keep away from her. Not because he was angry with her, but because he knew his resolve was weakening. It occurred to him, as his new valet was putting away his clothes, that he had no notion where Seph and her sister would be sleeping tonight.

'Roper, I can manage perfectly well on my own. I need you to discover where Miss Winterton and her sister are sleeping tonight.'

'I shall do so immediately, my lord.'

He returned looking worried. 'I have been unable to locate either her or her sister, my lord. Mrs Hopkins, who is back on duty, told me Susan has returned to her own room as she is feeling perfectly well. Miss Winterton's apartment is now available again.'

'Have you spoken to Lady Winterton?'

'Her ladyship has spent the day in her apartment and was not available. I spoke to her maid and the woman said Miss Winterton and Miss Charlotte have not visited since the morning.'

A flicker of unease ran through Ralph. 'What about the young gentlemen? Were you able to ask them?'

'I discovered them in the billiard room and they said they had not seen either of the young ladies today.'

His hands unclenched at this news. 'I'm sure there is a reasonable explanation for their absence. You must search the servants' quarters, including the staircases and passageways. Take someone with you who is familiar with this house. I shall search everywhere else.'

An hour later he was now very concerned for the safety of both girls. Was it possible they had gone outside and met with a mishap? It had been full dark for an hour or more and searching outside was going to be difficult, but he would not stop until he had found them.

'They have to have gone out . . . '

'Excuse me for interrupting, my lord, but I'm certain they didn't. I spoke to several of the grooms and they say no one from the house has been outside today. Two of them were clearing debris from the drive and would have seen them had they ventured that way.'

The girls appeared to have vanished into thin air. How could this be? There was one place he had not searched and that was the attics — not the occupied part where the servants resided, but the rest of the rooms, where discarded furniture and trunks of old clothes would be stored.

'Find me two lanterns. We are going to search the attics together.'

There was no point in alarming Lady Winterton at this juncture. He could think of no logical reason why the girls should have gone into the attics, but he must be sure. His search was fruitless and he could think of nowhere else to look. Then he remembered the many cellars beneath the house and the long dark passageways. He should have thought of this before; if they had gone down there they could well have become lost.

Roper fetched the two remaining footmen as they were familiar with the cellars. They all had a lantern. 'We must take a guide each, otherwise we might find ourselves lost.'

'Why should Miss Winterton and her sister wish to come down here, my lord?'

'I have no idea, but this is the only place we have not looked. They cannot have disappeared.'

After an unpleasant hour in the icy, dank conditions they had looked in every corner and found nothing. When they emerged in the warmth and light of the servants' rooms they were all chilled to the marrow. He was grateful for the mug of hot spiced wine that was handed to him by the housekeeper.

'Hopkins, I am now seriously concerned for their safety. How can two young ladies have disappeared so completely without anybody here seeing them go?'

'I have also organised a separate search. I can guarantee you they are not within these walls unless they somehow discovered a secret passage we know nothing about.'

His wine slopped over his hand. 'God's teeth!' He handed the half-drunk wine to her, beckoned to Roper, and thundered up the steps.

'There is a secret passage running from the drawing room to the apartment Sir Jeremy occupies. That is exactly the sort of place they would both wish to investigate. They must be trapped somewhere inside the walls of the house.'

He could not recall exactly which part of the panelling to press, so he ran to the old gentleman's quarters and hammered on the door.

His manservant opened it and immediately ushered him into the drawing room. 'Sir Jeremy, I need you to open your secret passage. I think Miss Winterton and her sister must be lost somewhere in the bowels of this house.'

The old man jumped to his feet. 'Good gracious me! How extraordinary! Come with me, my lord. I have been wandering about these passages since I was a boy and if they are indeed lost somewhere, I shall find them for you. I had no idea anyone but myself and my valet were aware of their existence.'

Ralph didn't wish to remind him how he knew. 'You two give your lanterns to Sir Jeremy and his man and return to your duties.' They did as he asked, leaving himself and Roper to accompany the other two.

'Wedge this panel open, Roper; it will let some light in.'

There was barely enough space for him to walk without becoming stuck, his shoulders were too broad for such a place. He turned slightly sideways and continued that way, awkward but efficient.

The illumination from four lanterns

was sufficient for him to see in all directions. Sir Jeremy paused when the passageway came to a junction. 'That way leads to a staircase and then to what used to be my bedchamber. This way continues to a flight of steps and then shortly after that it ends behind the stables. I shall go towards the chambers; I suggest you go the other way.'

How could the girls have become lost here? If they had not found a way to escape they would have returned to the drawing room and banged on the panelling until they attracted someone's attention. He was getting a very bad feeling about this.

They were certainly not anywhere within the confines of the passageway so, if they had actually come in here then there could be only one explanation. He increased his pace and almost fell head first down a slimy flight of steps. There was a door at the far end but even when he put his weight against it, it did not budge.

They would have to return to Sir

Jeremy's rooms. He had no need to explain to Roper, his man understood the urgency. They burst back through the panelling in the ground floor apartment to find their host waiting anxiously.

'They are not in there. The doors of both exits are locked. One emerges in the drawing room; get your man to show me where the other comes out.'

There was no argument on this point. The valet did not stop to put on his outdoor garments but led them through a side exit and onto the icy terrace. With his greatcoat swirling about his shoulders he ran after him and was gestured towards a small wooden door concealed by trailing ivy.

He tore this away and snatched open the door. Charlotte was crumpled on the floor. She was horribly silent and for a moment he thought her dead. There was no sign of his beloved. He dropped to his knees and his breath hissed through his teeth when he felt her cheek. It was cold but her pulse was strong.

'I have you safe now, little one, up

you come and I shall take you to your apartment where someone will look after you.' She stirred a little and her eyes flickered open as he was wrapping her snugly in his greatcoat.

'I was left here but they have abducted my sister. You must find her.'

'Never fear, she will be recovered safely. I know exactly who is behind this.'

*   *   *

The man who had dumped her had not spoken, but she knew who it was. At least, she knew it was either Defoe or Johnson for it could be no one else — both were large men and capable of carrying her about the place. She was bound as tight as a Christmas fowl but her fingers were free to move. This was a shed or outbuilding of some sort; there was dirt beneath her fingers, not boards or flagstones.

As her panic subsided she found she was able to breathe more freely, to think clearly again. The smell from the sack was not as noxious as she had at first thought, for it was horses she could smell. It had been used to transport fodder of some sort which was why the material was impregnated with dust and bits of straw. Her nose was almost clogged, she must remain calm because if she attempted to gulp in mouthfuls of air she was likely to swallow the debris and could well choke to death.

She had absolutely no doubt that Ralph would find her, that she would be released relatively unscathed. She would be able to bear her captivity more easily if she knew her sister to be safe somewhere. She tried to convince herself that they would not wish to hold both of them, so had in fact left Charlotte to find her own way back.

The cold and damp was seeping through her gown and petticoats. If she remained where she was, she was likely to freeze to death so she must somehow get to her feet and attempt to keep her limbs moving. Her back was hard against the rough brick of the wall and after a few failed attempts she was able to gain purchase with her feet. Slowly she inched her way upwards until she was standing straight.

The activity had warmed her a little but also made her breathing more difficult. She remained stationary until her heart stopped racing and her pulse slowed to a more normal pace. Before she had stood up, her arms had been pinned to the side. Now, there was some slack and she could twist her arms a little.

She moved them back and forth and as the blood began to flow again, so did her spirits rise. She had obviously been tied up when she was flat on the floor but standing meant the ropes were now looser. She put one arm in front of her, giving her another inch, and then she wriggled her left hand until she reached her neck and was able to push it through the last loop of rope.

She did the same with her right arm. The coil slithered down her body and she was able to step out. With considerable relief, she snatched off the sack and drew in half a dozen sweet mouthfuls of untainted air. She ran briskly on the spot until she was warm.

Her eyes had become accustomed to the semi-darkness and she made a quick examination of her prison. It was no more than two yards square so this did not take long. There were no windows and the walls were so thick she could not hear anything through them. There was a small amount of light filtering through a knothole in the door and she pressed her eye against it.

In the watery, winter sunshine she could see the area outside was deserted. There was no chance of attracting attention if she screamed. She shifted her position so she could look in all directions and came to the reluctant conclusion this must be somewhere away from both the house and the outbuildings attached to it.

She could no longer feel her extremities. If she was to survive this experience she must keep moving. Someone in her village had perished after falling, dead drunk, into a ditch one night and it had been less cold than it was now.

Everything that happened over the past days fell into place. The fact that the two gentlemen had been absent a lot of the time was now explained. They had been looking for somewhere to conceal her. The one thing that puzzled her was how they had learned about the secret passages — as far as she was aware, they had not spoken directly to Sir Jeremy. They could hardly be called secret if everybody knew how to enter and exit them.

Ralph must be searching for her now. She had convinced herself that her sister was safe and not part of this exchange. To think anything else would make her imprisonment impossible to bear. Would he hand over the letter without a second thought or would he try and negotiate?

What would she do in his position?

Would his safety matter more to her than handing secrets to the enemy? She hoped she would do the right thing as one life, however precious it might be, could not balance the scales against the lives of possibly thousands of British soldiers.

★   ★   ★

By the time Ralph had rushed through the house carrying his precious burden, word had gone upstairs. When he shouldered his way into the bedchamber, Hopkins and two maids were busily running a warming pan through the bed, and getting hot bricks wrapped in red flannel ready to go on either side of the girl.

She was now fully awake and he placed her gently on the daybed. He left her in the capable hands of the housekeeper and hurtled down the stairs to the study. He had thought of a way he could protect the letter and also rescue his darling girl without needing to break the necks of either man.

Roper followed him and watched with interest as he found a piece of similar paper. 'I am going to write some nonsense that will sound genuine and then give them this one instead.' He reached into his boot so he could see how the letter was set out, how many lines written and mimic the handwriting exactly.

'This will take me a little while. I assume that you have searched the billiard room for those two bastards?'

'I have, my lord. They are biding their time — they will be contacting you soon enough demanding an exchange.'

'Make sure they cannot access the stables. The doors must be barricaded from the inside and guarded by as many men as you can find who can handle a weapon. Good God, if it wasn't for the fact that Seph is their prisoner I would not hesitate to take them into custody right now.' He had been busily writing whilst talking and did not look up when his man replied.

'We can't arrest them if we don't

know where they are, my lord.'

'Very true, but at least one of them will show his face soon enough. You must take your lead from me. Until I have Miss Winterton safe we will not apprehend the one who comes to deliver the message.'

He did not have to state the obvious and say that the other would probably be standing with a pistol at Seph's head prepared to shoot her if necessary. Although he could see no profit in this for them. They would know he would hunt them down and kill them without compunction if they harmed a hair of her head.

He finished the facsimile, sanded it and folded it so it was exactly the same size as the original. He then put this back in his boot just in case his ruse was discovered and he had to hand this over as well.

'I am done. We must wait somewhere prominent and pray they come soon. It is too cold for her to be outside in her indoor clothes.'

13

Seph had found nothing to use as a weapon, the small bare room had been cleared of all debris. This was no coincidence, she was sure. Another more pressing problem was that she needed to relieve herself. She was not bothered about leaving a puddle in a corner but she was worried that she would be disturbed during the process.

She pressed her ear against the door and could hear nothing but silence. Emboldened by this she hurried to the furthest corner and did what was necessary. Behaving in such an unlady-like manner did not shock her, although she thought her grandmother would be scandalised if she was ever to hear about it, it gave her the courage to face whatever was coming.

Marching on the spot directly in front of the door meant she would hear the approach of anyone and would also keep the blood flowing around her limbs. As the house and park were so isolated there was no village with a church clock she could listen for and thus be able to keep track of the time.

It might seem to her she had been incarcerated for hours but realistically she thought it might only be one hour, possibly two, but no longer than that. Either rescue or one of her kidnappers must come soon. No sooner had she thought this than the hair on the back of her neck stood up. Someone was definitely approaching. It could not be rescue, as Ralph would be calling her name, so it had to be either Defoe or Johnson.

She could not ascertain whether the door opened inwards or outwards so she moved back to ensure she would not be knocked to the ground when they entered. The fact that they were carrying no lantern, were not speaking, must mean their perfidy had yet to be discovered.

There was the scraping sound of bolts being pulled back and then the door swung open. She could see nothing, had no idea who was there. Whoever it was did not speak but tossed something through the opening and then the door slammed shut.

Had they seen her standing there so had known she was well? Or had they just not cared about her well-being? She shuffled forward until her feet became entangled in material. She reached down and discovered whoever it was had given her not only a thick cloak to put on but also a blanket.

They obviously did not want her to perish from the cold which was a good sign. Gratefully she enveloped herself in the garment and then folded the blanket so she could sit on part of it and wrap the rest around her. She would resume her marching in a while but was now grateful to be sitting.

★ ★ ★

Ralph came face-to-face with the two men he was seeking. His pistol was out and he was pointing it with deadly accuracy. 'If you have harmed a hair on her head you will die today.'

Defoe and Johnson blanched and raised their hands immediately. No bravado, no threats and no demands to be given the letter.

'What the hell are you talking about, Didsbury? We have been playing billiards all afternoon and then returned to our chambers for some much-needed shut-eye,' Johnson said, his voice even, his eyes steady.

Roper was pressed close behind him and must have had his pistol pointed at Defoe.

'Miss Winterton and her sister were abducted. They were lured into the secret passageways . . . '

'Good God, man, you are talking in riddles. What secret passageways? Whatever you might think, this has nothing to do with us.'

For a moment he was undecided, and

then he lowered his weapon. 'If not you, then who?'

'The roads are open in the London direction, so it is possible we were followed here. Although God knows why they would abduct the young ladies — I can see no point in that.'

'Charlotte is unharmed and recovering in her room. Miss Winterton is still missing. We thought you had taken her and that you would use her to force me to give up the letter.'

The two exchanged a glance. 'You have it safe?' Defoe asked.

'I do. Until this moment I had not made up my mind about your role in this. Now I believe that you are who you say you are.' He delved into his boot and handed it over. 'I intended to take it to Horse Guards myself. If you were spies then I would have kept the information safe, if you were not then there could be no urgency about the matter.'

Why the hell were they talking about the letter when Seph was still missing?

He must resume his search at once.

'If we did not take her, then we must ascertain who did before we continue.' He led them to the study which he had taken over as his own. He was too agitated to speak seated, so the others remained on their feet too. He paced the room trying to make sense of what he knew. Then, suddenly, it was blindingly obvious.

'I don't think this is anything to do with you, I think it to do with Sir Jeremy.' He quickly explained the circumstances. 'I was puzzled as to how you could know about the secret passages but now I think it must be a member of the family who might well be aware of their existence.'

There was no need to tell them where they should be. As one, they left the study and thundered to the apartment in which the old man lived. He did not bother to knock; he strode in to find, to his surprise, no sign of distress, no unwanted intruders. His sudden appearance shocked Sir Jeremy.

Then he understood it was seeing Defoe and Johnson with him that had caused his host to turn pale.

'I beg your pardon, sir, but Miss Winterton has not been taken by these gentlemen as we thought, but we think by someone connected to you. How else would they know about the secret passages?'

He shrank back in his chair as if he had been struck. 'No one has approached me since the abduction. I have seen no strangers and would tell you if I had. I shall sign whatever they demand in order to obtain her release, do not concern yourself on that score.'

'You must do exactly the opposite. There are sufficient witnesses here for you to sign your new will and it will be legal. Then I shall take possession of it. This will give me the bargaining tool I need if necessary and leave you out of it.'

This was accomplished in minutes and he pushed the folded document into his inside pocket. 'I have not seen the girl who works for you here today. I wish to speak to her — she is the only one who could be in contact with these villains.'

'I have not seen her since this morning, my lord. She has a small room adjacent to the kitchen that my chef has been using these past two years.'

Ralph gestured to Roper and he took Johnson and vanished. 'We have no idea where Miss Winterton might be hidden. We have searched everywhere — is there somewhere no more than a mile away where she might be kept?'

'Have you looked in all the outlying buildings that are no longer in use?'

'They have been searched by your men and they found nothing.'

'Then I am at a loss to supply you with any further information. Perhaps your man will find something useful when he searches the girl's accommodation.'

Roper returned a few minutes later shaking his head. 'The room is empty, her belongings gone. She was definitely an accomplice in this.'

'Sir Jeremy, how long has she been employed here?' Ralph asked.

'She arrived at my door in September seeking employment. She told me she had been turned off by the squire and I had no reason to doubt her story. The man's son is notorious for mistreating the female staff and then getting them dismissed when they complain.'

'Defoe, Johnson, can I ask you to remain here with Sir Jeremy? Roper and I will question your chef. The girl might well have let slip something useful to him over the past months.'

'I take it you can vouch for the probity of your chef?'

'I put an advert anonymously in a London paper; he had to reply to a box number. He then had to journey to St Albans and speak to my lawyers and they sent him to me once they had vetted him. There is no possibility that he is linked in any way to my family.' He hesitated, looking uncomfortable, and then continued. 'However, I believe he is a conduit for correspondence from France to the émigrés living in this country. He is forever taking letters back and forth to the mail coach.'

Ralph looked at the two intelligence officers and they nodded. 'I'm sure there is nothing with which to concern yourself, sir.'

Johnson moved closer to the old man. 'Did you at any time see any of the letters he received from France? Or indeed, any of those that came from London to be posted on?'

'I did indeed. He sometimes read snippets from them and very amusing they were too. If I had thought for one moment he was a French spy I would have turned him in immediately. He was open in his interview that he wished to work for me so that he could send the letters to Dover. As there is no legitimate way to send letters out of the country he had to liaise with smugglers and so on in order to carry out his mission.'

'What he is doing is illegal, but I doubt anyone will wish to press charges and have him arrested.' He looked pointedly at Johnson and Defoe and they shrugged and smiled. 'Send for me at once if there is any communication from the abductors.'

His interview with the chef was brief. The man was just relieved he was not going to be sent to the assizes and gave his word he would discontinue the practice forthwith. Unfortunately, he had nothing pertinent to tell them about the missing girl. She had received, as far as he was aware, no letters or communications from anyone at all during her months at the house.

'I am going outside again, Roper, there must be an outbuilding the men failed to search properly. She might well not survive the night if we do not find her.'

'Shall I speak to the head groom and tell him he can unbarricade the stables?'

'Yes, and I want all the men out

searching with me again. They must bring lanterns.'

He could not recall where he had abandoned his, so removed one from a hook outside the stables. The temperature had dropped again. It was going to be a freezing night — not one to be shut in an unheated outbuilding with no blankets or outdoor garments for protection.

When the men were gathered in the flickering golden circle he explained his wishes. 'We must expand the search; Miss Winterton might be within a mile of here. I pray they did not have time to carry her any further before my men began to search the district. Roper, you take half the men and go to the right and I shall go to the left with the rest.'

He was still within hailing distance of the house when he heard his name yelled. He recognised the voice. It was Johnson calling him back. There must have been contact from the kidnappers.

⋆　⋆　⋆

Several unpleasant hours later, Seph heard someone approaching. She put her eye to the knothole and saw a man muffled in a scarf, with his hat pulled over his ears, holding up a lantern which was obscured on three sides so the light only shone in the direction it was pointed. She remained in position and waited.

The door opened and he gestured that she come out but she was not going anywhere. The only reason they could wish to move her was because her discovery was imminent.

'I am not going anywhere. You would be wise to flee because when my future husband finds you he will kill you without compunction.' Her voice was commendably steady despite the fact that her heart was hammering in her throat.

There was something about this man that bothered her but she could not decide what it was. He did not take kindly to her reply. She backed until she was against the far wall and he followed. He had seemed unsurprised to see her free of her restraints — but then he had known she was free when he tossed in the cloak and blanket earlier.

She could not see the point of him obscuring his face as she already knew who he was. Why did he not speak to her? Before she could form any conclusion, his fist moved and there was a searing pain in the side of her head and her world went black.

⋆   ⋆   ⋆

When she opened her eyes, it was dark. She must have been unconscious for a while. Her head ached horribly but she was not nauseous so was confident she had not suffered a concussion. This time she was lying on a makeshift bed and warmly covered with two blankets.

There was sufficient light filtering in from under the door for her to see around her prison. There was a bucket with a lid in one corner and beside her were a jug of water and a hunk of bread on a tinplate. They obviously did not intend her to freeze or starve, which contradicted the ferocity with which she had been struck down.

She used the rudimentary facilities with relief and then drank eagerly from the water. The bread was relatively fresh and she forced herself to eat although it kept sticking in her throat. After consuming barely a third she gave up.

There was a window and there were rough boards on the floor which made her think she was inside a building — perhaps a simple cottage in the neighbourhood. The bedding was surprisingly clean, no nasty surprises, and the room was vermin-free. With nothing to stand on, she could not gain the height she needed in order to look out and see where she was, although as it was night she would not be able to see anything anyway.

She tried the door and it was no surprise to find it firmly bolted. When she put her eye to a crack she could just discern the outline of a wooden settle, and could hear the murmur of voices, but too far away for her to hear what was being said. She was certain one of them was female. It must have been her who was making sure she did not perish during her incarceration.

She was still at a loss to understand why she had not already been exchanged for the letter. Also, why would the spies be taking so much trouble not to be recognised when she already knew who they were? She wandered about the room trying to make sense of it all.

Then she understood. She had not been taken by either Johnson or Defoe, but by someone else entirely. The only possible explanation was that her abductors had taken her in order to persuade Sir Jeremy to leave his estate to his unpleasant relative.

* * *

Ralph was accosted by Sir Jeremy the moment he set his foot inside the house. 'Quickly, quickly, come with me.'

His arm was grabbed and he was

obliged to accompany the old man whether he wished to or not. Once they were in the ground floor apartment he was released.

'Tell me at once what has happened.'

'I have had a note. I don't know how it came to be here as I did not see it come and neither did my valet.' He waved the missive and then shoved it into Ralph's hand.

We have Miss Winterton. She will not be released until you have given us a will leaving everything to your cousin Robert Wybrow.

You have until ten o'clock tomorrow morning. Bring the document to the deserted cottage where Miss Winterton was first held.

If you fail to comply you will not see her again.

'It must have been your girl who brought this here. Is there another entrance you have not told me about?'

'My man is looking for any open

windows and will return when he has discovered how this letter was delivered without us being aware of its arrival.'

Ralph patted his pocket. 'I have the genuine article, do you still have the original? The one where your fortune is left to your distant relative?'

'I do not. It was burnt the moment I returned and that new one written. I shall pen another . . . '

'Do that. You have made it perfectly clear in the one I have that if any other copies are presented to the lawyers they are invalid and have been written under duress. Do you recall what you had in the first?'

'Not exactly, but I can produce something similar. It will take me an hour or more. But we have until tomorrow so I think it's better that I make a good job of it and take my time.'

'I shall continue the search. I think it likely they have moved her further away by now.'

'Why should they do that, my lord?' Roper asked.

'We have now widened the search parameters and the fact that they can deliver a letter without being seen must mean they have someone close by watching what we are doing. We shall continue our search on horseback.'

Sir Jeremy had an irritating habit of grabbing his arm but Ralph was too polite to shake him off. 'My lord, I cannot apologise enough for bringing this woe down upon your shoulders. This is all my fault . . . '

'If you had not taken us in a few nights ago we would have perished. What has happened is unfortunate, but I attach no blame to you.'

★   ★   ★

The temperature had dropped again and the grass crunched under his boots. They had been riding for an hour when they came across a deserted farmhouse. When he lowered his lantern, he saw at once there had been someone there recently as the footprints were clear.

The horses clattering into the yard would have alerted anybody inside so there was no necessity for silence. 'Seph, shout back if you are here.' His voice echoed in the darkness; there was no reply.

He flung himself from the saddle and began to kick open doors. The fourth one, an outbuilding, was empty but it had been his beloved's prison until recently. He swung the lantern around and saw a discarded sack and ropes. A white-hot fury flooded through him. Whoever these people were, they would pay for what they had done to the woman he loved.

Flakes of snow began to drift past his face. Then it became heavier and the wind picked up.

'My lord, we must return to the house immediately or we will become lost in the blizzard,' one of the men yelled out to him.

With great reluctance he complied. He just had to pray those who held Seph had moved her somewhere more convivial and that she would survive the night. It was some consolation to believe that the abductors had nothing to gain if she died.

It should not have taken more than fifteen minutes to return directly to the stables but twice they missed their path even with a local man taking the lead. Eventually they clattered under the archway and their mounts were as relieved as they were to be home and out of the elements.

He checked and saw the other searchers were also back. 'Roper, we must abandon our hunt for tonight. I intend to go out at first light regardless of the weather. We can use the sledge in the carriage house that fetched the servants. There is a pair of horses better able to withstand such inclement weather than our thoroughbreds.'

The head groom overheard his remark. 'I shall have the sledge and the horses waiting for you at daybreak tomorrow, my lord.'

Ralph shrugged off his outer garments and tossed them to Roper who vanished up the back stairs to deal with them. Before he spoke to Sir Jeremy he had the unpleasant task of informing Lady Winterton and Charlotte that he had failed to return with Seph.

He went to her ladyship's sitting room first and was surprised, but pleased, to see the girl there too. Considering the circumstances, they both looked remarkably cheerful. Before he could speak the old lady raised her stick and waved it in the air. 'See here, my lord, this was pushed under the door an hour ago.' She nudged Charlotte and immediately she ran over and handed him a crumpled piece of paper.

Printed in almost illegible script were the words, 'SHE WILL BE WELL. SHE AIN'T IN NO DANGER.'

His eyes filled and he was almost unmanned at the relief that washed over him. 'I thank God for this note; I would have had a sleepless night otherwise. I take it you are aware why she has been kidnapped?'

'We are, young man, she is being held

ransom and will be exchanged for Sir Jeremy's will.'

'Exactly so. I wish I could have found her tonight, but what you might not be aware of, my lady, is that there is another blizzard blowing outside which made it impossible to continue the search for your granddaughter.'

'It will be the Lord's name day tomorrow. My granddaughter was to hold an informal service in the chapel. I am not pleased that this will not now take place. It is most inconvenient. I sincerely hope this matter has been resolved so we can have a service later in the day.'

He bit back his sharp retort. There was no point in antagonising her. It could be that she was hiding her worry by complaining about such trivialities — but he doubted it.

14

Nobody came in to speak to Seph and she was resigned to remaining here for the remainder of the night. Her accommodation was basic but at least she was warm enough and had a bed to sleep on. If it wasn't for the fact that she knew Ralph and Charlotte would be out of their minds with worry she could endure this without being too concerned. Her grandmother would just assume someone would bring her back safely. All her life she had relied on other people to put things right for her.

As there was nothing else to do she might as well make herself comfortable on the rudimentary bed. With her cloak wrapped around her and then the two blankets she was relatively comfortable. It must be at least nine o'clock, possibly later, so it would be Christmas Day before she was home with her family.

Sleep eluded her, despite being certain she was not going to be physically harmed. Her stomach gurgled and rumbled from lack of food and she had drunk all the water and was already thirsty again. As there was nothing else to do to occupy her, she decided to come to a firm decision about whether she should marry Ralph as soon as possible or remain with her original decision to wait until May.

She started with the positive points: handsome, strong, courageous, intelligent, kind — the fact that he was also a lord and wealthy came low on her list of reasons to marry him. The negative items: arrogant, dictatorial, fiery-tempered — however hard she thought, she could think of no further things that were in his disfavour.

Now she took into consideration his feelings for her, which were stronger than hers for him. Rather than being a problem, she thought this would make her life easier as he would be doing his best to win her over and probably allow her more freedom than he would have done otherwise.

From whichever way she looked at it she would be foolish indeed if she did not snatch his hand off in her eagerness to become his wife. The thought of sharing his bed and the intimacies that would take place there sent waves of heat around her body. This was one side of marriage she was eagerly anticipating. The fact that the result of this lovemaking should bring her children made her smile. A nursery full of little boys who looked like their father and little girls in her image would be a pleasure indeed. She was not so certain that daughters with dark red hair would be as delightful but as long as any progeny they were blessed with were healthy, she would not quibble.

She was woken the next morning by sounds of someone in the adjoining room making up the fire. She rolled out of bed and quickly used the primitive facilities. Her mouth was dry, her lips cracked and she had never been so hungry in her life. Were they not even going to give her water and bread today?

She glanced up at the window and saw to her horror it was thick with snow. How would Ralph find her now? Shortly after this she heard heavy footsteps approaching and braced herself. The door opened with a crash and facing her was the muffled man. He gestured with his head that she accompany him and she could see no reason to refuse.

Something prompted her to address him. 'There is no need to hide your face from me. I know you are either the relative of Sir Jeremy that he mentioned or someone working for him. I take it he has agreed to the exchange?'

Her captor shrugged and unwound the scarf that covered his face, revealing that he was a man of middle years, with grey hair and a deep scar running from his left eye to the corner of his mouth. Hardly reassuring.

'I ain't been comfortable keeping you

shut up like this, Miss Winterton. Here, take the seat near the fire and my lass will bring you something warm to eat.'

The girl who had let them into the house last week appeared a few minutes later with a tray. There was porridge and tea, not her usual fare, but she was so hungry she could eat anything with relish. She was unsurprised to find this girl was an accomplice. It all made perfect sense now the details were slotting into place.

'Thank you, I feel so much better now.' The girl handed her a toasting fork and a plate with three slices of bread. This was perhaps a foolhardy thing to do in the circumstances as the fork could be used as a weapon.

'There ain't no butter, miss, but there's dripping and it's real tasty.'

The man had covered his face and gone off into the snow, which allowed her to question the girl. 'When is the exchange to take place? How much snow has fallen overnight?' She was about to ask another question when she realised what day it was. 'It is the Lord's name day. This is hardly how I expected to be spending it.'

'Here's the dripping. I ain't supposed to talk to you. Me pa will tan me hide if he catches me.'

'He cannot possibly know as he is no longer here. Please answer my questions if you can.'

'The gent what is paying him is doing that at ten o'clock. I ain't sure what the time is, but it can't be more than eight now. There's a goodly amount of snow, right over me boots when I went out to use the privy.'

'Is this cottage on the estate?'

'It ain't, it's more than five miles from the house. Me pa has been living here this past month . . . '

'But surely, you have been working for Sir Jeremy longer than that.'

'I were happy there. I didn't know nothing about no wills when I took it, honest I didn't.'

'Then tell me how you became involved.'

'Sir Jeremy give me two days' leave and I went home. I told me pa what a right strange setup it were and I reckon somehow he got in touch with them men.'

'I am glad my abduction was not your doing. I shall do my best to keep you from being arrested but I warn you that when Lord Didsbury catches up with your father he might not survive the experience.'

'I took a note, I ain't much at writing, but I told your grandma you was safe.'

'How did you manage to get into the house without being seen?'

'That man, the man what wants to get Sir Jeremy's money for himself, told us about the secret passages. I ain't sure how he knew himself that they were there.'

'I suppose it was you that told my sister where to find the entrance?'

'I had no choice, miss, I'm that feared of both of them.'

'In which case we must escape

together. If you help me then I am certain his lordship will not wish to have you sent to jail.'

For a moment the girl hesitated then she nodded. 'I'll find me things whilst you finish up that toast. I'll take you to the church. It ain't no more than a mile across the fields and I reckon it'll be full of locals and they'll take care of you.'

'I shall take you into my employ if you would care to come with me when we leave?'

The girl beamed and curtsied. 'It would be more than I deserve, miss. I'll not let you down again.'

*　*　*

Ralph retired for a few hours but was up and ready to leave before dawn. He was determined to find Seph before the ten o'clock deadline. When she was recovered he could meet the abductors without fear and they would get the comeuppance they deserved.

'Roper, ensure there are furs and

blankets in the sledge. They will be needed.'

Despite the hour, the head groom had the horses harnessed and each one was snugly covered with a thick rug. They were hairy-legged beasts with shaggy coats and perfect for the appalling weather. He had intended to send word to the nearest magistrate that the militia should be raised or at the very least a constable sent to detain the villains when he had finished with them.

The vehicle had room for two on the driver's box and there would be accommodation for four inside. The only drawback was that the sledge was open to the elements. Thank God it was no longer snowing. There were sacks draped across the squabs to keep them free from any snow falling from the trees as they passed. There was now a pile of rugs and blankets in the well of the sledge; these were also covered with clean sacks.

He was driving himself and knew

exactly where he was going. Sir Jeremy had told him there was a small village a few miles away and there were outlying cottages that would be ideal for hiding Seph. He snapped the whip in the air and the horses threw their weight into the traces and the sledge moved forward slowly.

'God's teeth! I had forgotten it is Christmas Day. This is not how I expected to be spending it.'

'The Almighty will understand that rescuing Miss Winterton must come first.' Roper was almost unrecognisable beneath the muffler, cap and heavy-caped riding coat with which he was covered. No doubt he looked equally odd as he was similarly attired.

The horses plodded forward willingly and even though the snow was inches deep in places, they made light work of it. The sun was slowly rising and the snow made it seem lighter than it was. The blizzard had passed during the night but it was still bitterly cold. From his vantage point he could see across the hedges, and the spire of the village church was just visible in the distance.

'I shall head towards the church. It is the perfect landmark as I can see it clearly even though I cannot see the village itself.'

Roper was obliged to get down a couple of times in order to open and close gates. They were travelling across the fields with no difficulty. The return journey would be simpler as it would be full light and they would be able to follow their tracks.

Eventually they emerged onto a narrow lane and with some difficulty he turned the horses towards the huddle of cottages in the distance. There was sufficient light for him to grope beneath his outer garments and remove his pocket watch from his waistcoat. He flicked the cover open.

'It is a little after eight o'clock, Roper, not too early to wake the residents and make enquiries. I need to know if there have been any strangers seen in the area and if so where they are residing.'

His man already had a pocketful of coins with which to reward anyone who gave them useful information.

'I reckon you can turn in front of the church up there. It will be more sheltered too.'

Ralph nodded and waited for him to climb down before urging the team in the direction of the church. They appeared as fresh and eager to go as they had been an hour ago — there was something to be said for having common horses in the stable as well as thoroughbreds. These were not as tall as farm horses or as lean as his team, but somewhere in between.

He pulled the handle that applied the brakes to the runners and then wrapped the reins around the post. He clambered down and went to check each of their hooves. He used the knife he always carried tucked into his boot to remove the compacted snow. Satisfied the animals would be able to return without discomfort, he adjusted their rugs and gave them each a half of a wrinkled apple he had brought with him for this very purpose.

He stamped his feet and looked towards the empty building. What time would the curate come to light the candles? There would be a service this morning, and would have been one at midnight last night, but he had no idea exactly when this would be. He might as well sit on the box where at least he could see anyone approaching.

With the fur around his knees he would be warm enough. Slowly he swivelled on the box so he could see in all directions. A movement in a field a long way behind the church caught his eye. He stood up in order to get a better view. His heart pounded. There were two figures, both female, trudging towards the church and he was certain that one of them was his beloved Seph.

There was a gate through which he could drive the horses and fortunately it was open so he did not have to climb down to open it. Once he was in the first pasture he could no longer see over the hedge to the second field where the girls were. He snapped his whip and urged his horses faster. They could not trot, the snow was too deep, but they walked more quickly and he could ask no more of them.

He secured the reins to the post so they would continue in the same direction, removed the rug from his knees and carefully got to his feet so not only would he be able to see into the field beyond but would also be visible to Seph and her companion.

★ ★ ★

After the girl had slipped several times, Seph had linked her arm through Betty's. She was taller and stronger and hoped she could keep her upright on the journey. The snow had stopped, thank the good Lord, but the wind was biting and as they progressed into the centre of the field it became colder and more difficult to walk.

Then to her astonishment she heard

Ralph call her name. She stopped in her tracks and looked towards his voice. He was somehow suspended above the hedge waving frantically at her and then he disappeared.

'Well I never! His lordship has come to fetch us. It is a Christmas miracle, that's what it is.'

'Quickly, Betty, he must have fallen from whatever he was standing on. I am concerned he has hurt himself.'

'He wouldn't come to no harm, Miss Winterton, not falling into the snow like what he did.'

A minute ago they had been exhausted; now, her energy returned and she was able to almost run towards the gate. As they approached, two equine heads appeared, ears pricked, steam puffing from their nostrils, nodding as if encouraging them to hurry. There was still no sign of Ralph.

Then she heard him approaching. 'Move aside, stupid animals, I cannot open the gate if you are standing so close to it.'

269

'There is no need to, my lord, we can climb over perfectly well.'

There was a deal of bad language spoken before her beloved was able to force himself between the horses, which showed no inclination to move.

Seph almost hurled herself over the gate and into his arms. He crushed her to him and she welcomed his kisses.

'Are you unharmed, my love? I have been out of my mind with worry since you were taken.'

She rested her cheek against his snow-smothered coat, too overcome with emotion to speak. She gathered herself and looked up at him, her eyes brimming. 'Betty set me free. I was initially in unpleasant circumstances but spent the night warm and fed. Her father forced her to participate in my abduction. He and the hopeful heir to Sir Jeremy's estates are the real villains. I beg you to allow her to work for us as I gave her my word she would not be arrested.'

He rubbed her cheeks dry with his thumb. 'Then she shall not be. Come, we cannot leave the horses standing. The two of you climb into the sledge and cover yourselves with the rugs. I shall turn the team and then we can collect Roper as we go through the village.'

Soon she and her new maid were snug under the covers, Ralph was back on the box and they were on their way home. His man scrambled on board and they left the village behind just as the church bells began to ring. The sun reflected off the snow, making the world seem magical.

The sledge glided along smoothly and the horses increased their pace when they were turned towards their stable. She leaned back on the squabs and enjoyed the ride. Perhaps it was not too late to celebrate the Lord's name day with a service in the chapel?

They were back in no time at all and she was almost sad the ride was over. The first thing she must do was speak to her family, the second was to have a thorough wash and change her garments. Then she would be ready to lead the prayers and the day could unravel as planned.

Ralph was off the box before the sledge was stationary and was there to lift her out before Betty had finished removing the furs and blankets. The happy words she had been about to utter dried in her throat. She did not recognise the man who placed her on the cobbles. His expression was hard, his eyes like green flint, and he did not spare her more than a cursory glance.

She was about to remonstrate when he spoke. 'Inside, Seph, and remain upstairs until I give you leave to come down.' He pushed her almost roughly towards the open door and she had no option but to obey. She was seething, determined to tell him what she thought, when suddenly she understood his behaviour.

Now she was safe, he intended to deal with the perpetrators. She sent up a fervent prayer that no one would die today of all days. She was not sure she could marry him if he had blood on his hands, whatever the justification.

15

Ralph needed to focus all his attention on the forthcoming confrontation. It was now almost half an hour past nine o'clock. It belatedly occurred to him that whoever was watching the house might already know Seph was home safe and that they had no bargaining tool. This surely meant there would be no meeting after all.

He patted his pocket to check his gun was there. Roper was tacking up two horses. The sledge was too cumbersome for this journey. He had been brusque with his darling girl and she had been dismayed by his formality, but she would understand when this was over.

The clatter of hooves behind him meant the mounts were ready. Again the head groom had found horses up to their weight but of a more sturdy constitution than he was accustomed to. He was about to swing into the saddle when he reconsidered. 'I think this a pointless exercise. I have no wish to confront these villains now that Miss Winterton is safe. If they have any sense, the two men will make themselves scarce before I can set the militia on them.'

His man looked relieved. 'I reckon it would be a wasted journey, my lord.'

With a smile Ralph handed the reins back to him and strode into the house. There was still time to make this Christmas Day memorable, but for the right reasons this time. He met the housekeeper in the hall.

'Hopkins, is the chapel ready for the prayer meeting?'

'It is, sir. Is Miss Winterton well enough to conduct the service for us? The staff are eager to pay their respects to our Lord on his anniversary.'

'Convey this message to Sir Jeremy; tell him that everything is resolved satisfactorily. We shall be there for prayers in an hour. I suggest that the staff break their fast now and then you can serve us in the breakfast room afterwards.'

He glanced around the hall. 'If there are sufficient candles I should like them grouped around the place.'

The woman almost smiled. 'There is a holly tree in the kitchen garden, my lord, would it be in order to pick some and arrange it around the candles to give the place a festive air?'

He nodded. 'Yes, that would be most acceptable. I have a lot to be thankful for this Christmas and so does Sir Jeremy, so I am sure he will not object to the added expense.'

Roper had taken to his new position as valet in a most efficient way and stepped forward to remove Ralph's outer garments as if he had been doing it all his life. 'I shall need to wash and shave and change but first I must speak to Miss Winterton. Have everything arranged for my return.'

He bounded up the stairs and headed for Lady Winterton's rooms. He could hear excited voices behind the door and knocked loudly. The door was flung open by Charlotte who looked somewhat surprised to see him.

He stepped around her, ignored the bad-tempered old lady and snatched up Seph and carried her from the room before she could protest at his high-handed treatment. He shouldered his way into his own sitting room and placed her gently on her feet.

'I apologise if I was less than polite a few moments ago. My intention had been to teach those villains a lesson but I decided I was content to have you back unscathed and would leave their punishment to the proper authorities.'

She tilted her head to one side and pursed her lips as if not sure whether she was pleased to see him or not. 'I do not like being sent to my room like a recalcitrant child, Ralph. I hope this is not a precedent you have set.'

He grinned and pushed an errant strand of hair from her face. 'I hope you forgive me for saying so, my love, but you are in dire need of a good wash. The staff will be gathering in the chapel in less than an hour and we need to be in our best apparel.'

She laughed and, as always, this made his pulse race. 'I think that is the case of the pot addressing the kettle. You look like a very grubby brigand. I shall leave you to your ablutions and shall return to my own apartment to take care of mine.'

Before she could slip away he caught her hand and drew her close. Their kisses were tender, loving, and he knew in that moment that her feelings had changed, that she loved him as he did her. Reluctantly he released her and she ran gracefully from the room.

They were once more cut off from the world but as soon as it was safe to travel he would take his future wife and her family to his home. The banns could be called the first Sunday and then they could be married by the end of January. He rather thought that most young ladies required several weeks to put together their bride clothes but he doubted this would be the case with Seph. He would open his townhouse in Hanover Square and he would employ the best seamstress to make whatever she desired.

Then if she so wished they could remain for the Season, bring out her sister in London after all, or return to Kent. Two weeks ago, the thought of attending an overcrowded ballroom, a rout or a soiree, had filled him with horror; now his opinion had changed. Escorting his beautiful new wife, and introducing her to society, would bring him nothing but pleasure.

Once he was suitably attired he went in search of Seph and her family. They were, remarkably, ready before him. In his experience, ladies of any age could be expected to take twice as long as a gentleman to get ready.

'Lady Winterton, would you like my assistance on the stairs?'

'It would be so much easier to be carried. I thank you, my lord.'

He had only intended to take her arm but he was happy to do as she wished. She handed her cane to Charlotte and looked expectantly at him. He scooped her up and he was shocked at how little she weighed. He had thought her a stout woman but her bulk was misleading and was obviously made by the amount of petticoats she wore.

He placed her gently on her feet, keeping his arm around her waist until she had her stick in her hand. 'That was most enjoyable, sir, could I prevail upon you to repeat the process in reverse when I wish to retire?'

'I should be delighted, my lady.'

'Seph, do you know where the chapel is? I know there is one, but I have not come across it.'

'We shall follow my grandmother as she has already made use of it.'

The place of worship used by the family was tucked away in the west wing. It had seats for a dozen and standing room for a dozen more. The altar was a simple table upon which a large brass cross stood. There was even a pretty coloured glass window depicting the Last Supper.

Sir Jeremy, Johnson and Defoe were there before them. The gentlemen stood until the ladies were seated. Then he glanced over his shoulder to see all the inside staff had also gathered behind the chairs. He bowed his head, as did everyone else, and they sat in silent prayer for a few minutes.

Seph moved to the front of the small chapel and faced the congregation. She then read several pertinent passages from the Bible, said two prayers and then led them in the Lord's Prayer. The staff dispersed and he turned to Lady Winterton.

'Do you wish me to take you back to your apartment now?'

She stared at him as if he was a lunatic. 'Good heavens, young man, have you lost your senses? I might be decrepit, but I do not retire before I have broken my fast.' She stomped off in the direction of the breakfast parlour and he found himself walking beside Sir Jeremy. The girls were together as were the other two gentlemen.

'Lord Didsbury, I have sent word to the constable about the abduction. I was shocked to hear that Miss Winterton has decided to employ the girl who used to work for me. I must insist that the girl be sent away at once. I will not have her under my roof.'

Ralph was about to give a pithy reply but reconsidered. He had been treating this as if it were his own home, which it wasn't. 'We shall be leaving at first light tomorrow, and I'm sure you would not wish the girl to be turned out into the snow before then. If it had not been for her bravery, Miss Winterton would not be here now and things might be very different.'

* * *

Seph, unknown to the two of them, had been eavesdropping on this conversation. To interrupt would be the height of bad manners but she had no choice.

'Excuse me, Sir Jeremy, but I could not help overhearing what you said about Betty. The girl left your employ and when she did so she was no longer any concern of yours. She is now with me; therefore, it is my decision whether I dismiss her. I will not be doing so and neither will I leave here when there is so much snow on the ground that travelling would be dangerous.'

Ralph shook his head slightly but she ignored him and continued. 'Let me remind you, sir, that my abduction was directly related to your business. If we had not been here then you would already have been forced to sign away your fortune. I believe that Lord Didsbury has also put that matter right.'

There was no need to say anything else as she had made her point beautifully. As there was now a gap between Ralph and Sir Jeremy, she sailed through, her sister close beside her, and was able to enter the breakfast room just behind her grandmother.

As usual she and Charlotte collected what their ancient relative wanted and took the two plates to the table, where she was now sitting waiting eagerly for her food. There was coffee, chocolate and tea on the table and she poured a bowl of chocolate before returning to the buffet to select her own repast.

Mr Johnson and Mr Defoe strolled in and waited politely for her sister and herself to finish before beginning their own choice. Where were Ralph and Sir Jeremy? For a second she thought she would abandon her meal and go in search of them but she was too hungry to do that.

The conversation around the table was mainly about the inclement weather, the delicious dinner they were to have in honour of the day, and the where-abouts of their host and Ralph.

Neither of them had come in by the time she had finished her substantial meal. There was something untoward taking place and no doubt it was her fault. She must really learn to hold her tongue if she was not to cause further disharmony.

'Persephone, I am replete. I shall sit in the drawing room and you may play a hand of Whist with me until I wish to retire for my afternoon rest. What has happened to Lord Didsbury? I require you to find him so that I may be sure he will be available when I wish to go up.'

'Grandmama, you are perfectly able to climb the stairs without being carried about like a parcel. I am more concerned that neither gentleman has eaten any breakfast. Ralph has been gallivanting about the countryside since before dawn and must be ravenous.'

There was a footman standing with his back to the wall pretending he was invisible. She thought it remarkable how quickly the two outside men had adapted to inside rules. 'Find Lord Didsbury.'

The young man nodded and hurried out. She had not told him what to do when he had this information, which was foolish of her. Too late to repine

— she would not exacerbate matters by going in search of him herself so had no recourse but to accompany her sister and grandmother to the drawing room.

However, she refused to play cards when she was so anxious. She settled the other two on either side of the card table and then changed her mind about searching for Ralph. The footman had not returned which was a very bad sign.

Was it possible Sir Jeremy would demand that they left this very day? He did not have the resources to physically evict them but he could, she supposed, use the threat of dismissing the entire staff if they did not leave. She had thought him a benevolent old gentleman, but obviously she had been sadly mistaken in this assessment. Ralph had said the old man was to accompany them to Didsbury — would this still be the case?

'Charlotte, I trust you to take care of our grandmother. I have an errand to run.' She did not have far to go before she came face-to-face with her betrothed.

One look at him was enough to tell her he was most displeased with her. She was not going to receive a set-down where her family could overhear it. 'Shall we go to the study, my lord? We can be private there.'

Not waiting for him to disagree, she all but ran down the passageway and into the chamber. The fire had obviously been lit early as the room was delightfully warm, unlike the passageways. Only the vast entrance hall was not icy and unpleasant to walk through.

She moved into the centre of the room and looked around for a suitable chair. The door closed with a decided snap behind her and her heart sank to her boots. Wearing outdoor footwear beneath her pretty gown would be considered the height of inelegance but she cared not for that. Having been so cold and uncomfortable for twenty-four hours, from now on she would wear items that suited the conditions.

'I hope you are pleased with yourself.' He spoke from directly behind her when she had thought him still by the door. She swore her feet left the carpet and her bladder almost emptied. This was exactly the sort of thing she most disliked. She spun and found herself no more than an inch away from him.

Heat radiated from him and instantly her traitorous body reacted. She was burning, hot all over and could not prevent herself swaying into his arms. They closed around her and for a blissful few minutes she forgot everything but the feel of his lips on her mouth. He trailed his kisses down her cheek, into the hollow of her neck and lower. If he had not been supporting her she would have collapsed from the pleasure of it.

Then, abruptly, he stepped away and went to sit behind the desk. She remained rooted to the spot for a second and then almost staggered to the nearest seat and collapsed into it.

'I had no idea that being kissed was so exhausting,' she said as she curled her feet under her bottom and made herself comfortable. 'I can see why such activities would be better performed in bed.'

His shout of laughter made her jump for a second time. She glared at him but he gave her one of his wicked smiles and she realised the implication behind what she had said.

'I am thought to be a sensible sort of young lady, yet when I am in your company I say the silliest things and behave quite out of character. If you wish to break off the engagement now that you know me, I shall not hold you to it.'

'The more I get to know you the more I love you. You are exasperating, that is true, but you're also adorable, desirable and the most beautiful woman I have ever seen.'

This last compliment was too much and she laughed. 'I will accept the first two but not the third. I can only think that you are blinded by your feelings, my love, because I am no more than passable and well you know it.'

'I refuse to discuss this point. I am

Lord Didsbury and my opinion is always correct. Now, are you not eager to hear why I was obliged to miss my much-needed breakfast?'

'I was coming in search of you. I should not have . . . '

'No, sweetheart, you should not have but you spoke from the heart so I shall no doubt forgive you. I must add, however, that I do not expect you to make a habit of this as I shall not be so accommodating next time.'

'I shall do my best to be an obedient and well-behaved wife, but I cannot promise. Please, Ralph, tell me what has transpired. I shall not dismiss Betty so do not ask me to.'

'I have no intention of doing so and you will be relieved to know I have convinced Sir Jeremy that the girl is to be congratulated for what she did. Once he had the full story — which I got from her myself — he accepted that she was coerced into her behaviour and had not revealed his presence deliberately.'

'So, none of us are to be turned out into the snow on Christmas Day?'

'No, we are not.' He smiled as the unmistakable sound of a tray laden with rattling crockery approached the study. 'Excellent, my food is arriving. Will you keep me company whilst I eat? We have much to discuss about our future life together and I am certain you must have questions.'

They talked companionably until Ralph was summoned to transport her grandmother for her afternoon rest. 'I think I too shall take the opportunity to sleep. I had precious little last night and I wish to be fully alert for the celebration dinner that is planned for this evening.'

'In which case, darling girl, once I have returned her ladyship to her boudoir I will get some shut-eye too.'

They parted on the best of terms outside their respective bedchambers and he promised to collect her at five o'clock, after he had carried her grandmother down to the drawing room.

Charlotte joined her in bed. They

both disrobed and slipped under the covers in their petticoats. As she was drifting off to sleep it occurred to her that nobody knew for sure whether the kidnappers had actually left the area. Her stomach plummeted. Ralph had assured her they would go, that they had lost their gamble and would not risk losing their lives as well by being arrested.

Her lips curved at her wild imaginings. It had certainly been an exciting few days and she could not remember having been so happy in her life before.

Tonight, she would tell him that she returned his feelings and would be happy to marry him as soon as it could be arranged. It was strange that this subject had not come up during their conversation earlier; one would have thought it the first thing he would have wanted to know. Instead he had described the magnificent house she would soon be mistress of, his plans for their trip to London and suggestions for their wedding trip when the weather improved.

16

Ralph was fully recovered when he awoke a few hours later. Roper had his evening rig laid out for him and he was able to carry Lady Winterton downstairs and return to collect his beloved in good time for dinner. He paused at the top of the stairs and turned to admire the hall. The housekeeper had found hundreds of candles and added a variety of bows and greenery to the groupings. It made this space look magical and he could not wait to share it with Seph.

As he strolled towards their apartment, Defoe and Johnson emerged from their rooms. 'Good God! Your ensembles are blindingly bright, gentlemen. But at least the ladies cannot say you have not made an effort.'

Defoe grinned. 'A silver brocade jacket with purple and gold striped waistcoat is not exactly to my taste, but it fits well enough. What do you think of Johnson?'

'Do you want the truth?' They both laughed. 'You look even worse than your friend. Was there really nothing else but gold, silver and purple to be found in the trunk that you were loaned?'

'Unfortunately not. I can assure you that these are the least gaudy we could find. It is hard to credit that Sir Jeremy in his youth was a macaroni.'

Ralph raised his hand in salute and they walked off, leaving him free to knock on the door. It was opened by Charlotte. 'We are ready, my lord . . . '

'Enough of the formality, Miss Winterton; you must call me Ralph as your sister does. We will be related very soon.'

The girl was looking stunning in a simple evening gown of some flimsy material the colour of butter and a darker gold underskirt. It was the perfect contrast for her colouring. He looked past her with a smile, searching for the woman he loved.

For a second, he was baffled and did not recognise her in her finery. Her hair had been arranged in an elaborate style, her remarkable eyes sparkled more than usual and the gown she was wearing was even more spectacular than her sister's. He held out his hand and she ran to him. He gathered her close and kissed the top of her head.

'You look beautiful, I think that gown is utterly lovely.'

'I have never worn it before. I shall tell you a secret — it was originally a gown belonging to my grandmother but I made it into the modern fashion. Emerald green is rather dashing for an unmarried lady, but I'm told that it complements the colour of my eyes.' She fluttered her lashes in a provocative way and he almost lost his control.

'You are fishing for compliments, sweetheart, but will have no more from me.' His future sister-in-law fluttered past, leaving them alone, which was perhaps unwise in the circumstances. 'Have you come to a decision about our nuptials?'

'Despite my determination not to, I find that I now am hopelessly in love with you. I cannot wait to be married and the ceremony can take place as soon as it can be arranged.'

He was about to kiss her when there was the hideous sound of a gunshot. 'Stay here, I shall deal with this.'

He was out of the room in seconds. Roper met him in the corridor and handed him a loaded, primed pistol. 'Them varmints must be here.'

Charlotte was crouched on the floor at the top of the stairs. 'Join your sister in the sitting room and remain there.' She needed no second bidding and scrambled to her feet and vanished.

There could have been no more than a minute or two since the first shot and he was waiting for a second, for raised voices, but the house was unnaturally quiet. Perhaps it would not be wise to hurtle down the stairs waving his gun but to proceed with caution, to see what was taking place before he appeared.

He backed away from the main staircase and together they ran to the secondary one. It was still too quiet.

'Secret passage — we can hear what's going on from there without being seen.'

Sir Jeremy's drawing room was empty but Ralph remembered how to open the panel. He grabbed the nearest candlestick, as did Roper, and they stepped into the darkness. The panel closed with a click behind them. It was difficult to run in so cramped a space but he managed it. When they reached the main drawing room he slowed his pace and pushed his ear to the wood.

At first he could hear nothing but then he heard Defoe speak. 'What can you possibly hope to gain by breaking in here like this? Even if you kill Sir Jeremy you will not inherit, the new will is on its way to his lawyers as we speak. They will ratify it tomorrow when they return to work.'

A different voice replied, one he had not heard before. 'Then he will write another which will supersede the one that is on its way. If he does not then my next shot will be into either you or your friend. I suggest that you persuade him if you wish to survive.'

'You are forgetting something: there are only two of you and a dozen armed men are waiting for my signal.'

Ralph had no idea how to open this panel but he had heard enough to prepare him. He backed away until he was certain he could not be heard when he spoke. 'They have two shots, as do we. We need to make them count.'

'Are there armed men, my lord?'

'We shall see when we get back into the main part of the house.'

He was met by Sir Jeremy's valet who was indeed holding a musket. 'There's four more men with guns, sir. I reckon we can overcome them easy enough.'

'Indeed we can, but we must do it without anyone but the intruders being harmed.' He thought for a moment. 'Roper, you and I are going to cause a distraction. Once they have discharged their weapons you can overwhelm them without the necessity of firing yours.'

He had no idea what it was going to take to draw their attention so that they fired their pistols but did not actually hit either himself or Roper. He would improvise when the moment came. He trusted in the Almighty to keep him safe — after all, had he not brought Seph to him in this extraordinary manner? If they were intended to be together then he would not be shot today.

His lips curved at his nonsense. He was not a religious man; he merely paid lip service to the church, so thought it highly unlikely there was a Supreme Being watching over his activities. If this being existed then he would have more important things to do than that.

As they crept towards the drawing room he spotted the dinner gong. This would be ideal. There was a second entrance to the drawing room at the far end which connected with the dining room. He sent Roper in that direction with two of the other men whilst he silently approached the entrance to the drawing room that was in the hall.

One of the footmen now had the gong. He gestured that he take it to the far side of the double doors. On his signal he flung both doors open and the man hammered on the gong as if his life depended on it. The clanging was sufficient to cause both men to swing round and gave Roper and the others their opportunity.

Whilst this continued, Ralph stepped into the room and fired his gun above the heads of the intruders. The combined racket caused the old lady to have a fit of the vapours, Sir Jeremy to drop his head in his hands but Defoe and Johnson surged to their feet and in seconds it was over.

The would-be assassins were knocked senseless, tied hand and foot and carried away to be dumped in one of the cellars until they could be collected by the constable and his men after Christmas.

'That was capital, my lord, I could not have done anything better myself.'

He grinned and went to yell up the stairs in a most ungentlemanly way that the two girls could now safely join them. The dinner gong was returned to its rightful place and order was restored.

Champagne was served in crystal glasses and a toast was drunk to celebrate the Lord's name day, his betrothal to Seph, and a successful conclusion to Sir Jeremy's problems.

Dinner was announced and they made their way into the dining room which had been beautifully decorated, the table laid with the best crystal and silverware and everywhere glowed in the candlelight.

'This looks absolutely beautiful, I cannot believe that Hopkins has been able to arrange things so well and in so short a time,' she exclaimed.

'I intend to keep the house open and

everyone who is employed here presently will remain. You have not seen my estate at its best, Miss Winterton, I hope that you and your future husband will visit again in the summer.'

She was about to answer when Lady Winterton interrupted. 'Do not include me in this invitation, sir, for I declare I shall never set foot here again in my lifetime. Two guns being fired in your drawing room is the height of bad manners.'

Charlotte giggled. 'You are quite right, Grandmama, and such a dreadful smell of cordite too. It is really too much, and on Christmas Day as well.'

Satisfied she had made her point, the old lady stomped to the table and waited to be seated. Sir Jeremy took the place next to her, the two gentlemen sat together and Charlotte joined them, leaving the remaining two seats for Ralph and Seph.

The upsets of the past week were forgotten when the magnificent first course arrived. There were a dozen removes, each one as delicious as the other. Ralph was enjoying a tasty morsel of chicken in herb sauce when his beloved touched his knee.

For a young lady to do such a thing was outrageous and he almost choked. She had obviously done this inadvertently. He glanced down at her, expecting her to be embarrassed, but the reverse was true.

'Yesterday I could have died; today the same could have happened to you. Therefore, I have made a decision. I do not wish to wait until we are married to share your bed.'

His cutlery clattered to his plate, causing several heads to turn. For the first time in his life he was unable to speak. Eventually he recovered his aplomb. Whilst he had struggled to respond she had been watching him closely, her eyes alight with laughter.

'I do not think you have thought this through, my darling. I'm sure you have no wish for our first child to be born several weeks earlier than it should be.'

302

'I believe that if you send Roper to find the nearest bishop you can obtain a licence and we can be married anywhere we please. Even in this inclement weather I believe he could make the journey there and back within a week.'

'Then that is what I shall do. You do realise that your sister will be aware . . . '

Her eyebrows shot up and her mouth rounded. 'Good heavens, I was not suggesting you joined us in my bed. I shall come to you.'

He shook his head. 'My love, you are outrageous. However, if you are absent from the bed you share with Charlotte, I am sure she is not so innocent she will not know why you are missing.'

'There you are wrong; as long as I am back before she wakes she will know nothing. Once she is asleep I believe you could fire a gun over her head and she would still not rouse.'

His appetite had deserted him despite the array of tempting plates on the table. The rest of the meal was interminable and he noticed that she barely touched the food. When the final cover was taken away she stood up and her grandmother and sister followed suit.

'Young man, I wish to retire to my bed immediately. You will take me up now if you please.' She turned her beady eye to Seph. 'Bring your sister up, she is inebriated and must retire immediately.'

When he returned Defoe and Johnson were waiting to speak to him. 'The snow has begun to melt for a second time. We shall leave at first light. I doubt that we shall meet again, my lord, but suffice it to say you have served your country well.' Johnson offered his hand and he took it willingly.

'Godspeed, and good luck with your future enterprises. This has been an extraordinary few days — life-changing for all of us.'

Although the hour was early he had no intention of lingering downstairs drinking brandy or waiting for a tea trolley. He bid them good night and bounded up the stairs.

Roper was waiting for him. 'Are we to leave tomorrow, my lord?'

'We are, but not until mid-morning. You must resume your responsibilities as coachman until we are back, but then I should like you to be my valet if you would still care to take that position?'

'I should indeed, sir. I shall leave out your travelling clothes as I will not be here to assist you to dress if I am to ready the carriage. Do you wish me to oversee Miss Winterton's carriage too?'

'Yes, that would be sensible. She will travel with me, the girl she has employed must travel with Lady Winterton and her sister.'

'I have already packed your trunk and had it conveyed downstairs so it can be loaded in the morning. Betty has done the same for Miss Winterton and Miss Charlotte. I shall have time to pack what remains whilst you breakfast.'

He dismissed his man and checked the bedchamber was warm, the bed too, and then stripped off his clothes. He looked for his bedrobe but it was no longer on the end of the bed. He could hardly greet his future wife as he was. Seeing a man unclothed for the first time might well make her change her mind.

His evening shirt would have to do. He was reaching for this when a prickle of awareness ran down his spine. He was not alone. The thought that she could see him naked made his pulse hammer. He dare not turn.

'Darling, do not put your shirt on for me. My nightgown has now joined it on the floor.'

★   ★   ★

When Charlotte awoke the next morning to find her sister missing she immediately thought that their grandmother had been taken ill in the night. She ran next door to find this was not the case. 'Go back to your rooms, child, your sister is with Lord Didsbury. There is nothing for you to worry about.'

THE RECLUSIVE DUKE
A LORD IN DISGUISE
CHRISTMAS AT DEVIL'S GATE
A MOST DELIGHTFUL CHRISTMAS
CHRISTMAS GHOSTS AT THE PRIORY

We do hope that you have enjoyed reading this large print book.

Did you know that all of our titles are available for purchase?

We publish a wide range of high quality large print books including:
Romances, Mysteries, Classics
General Fiction
Non Fiction and Westerns

Special interest titles available in large print are:
The Little Oxford Dictionary
Music Book, Song Book
Hymn Book, Service Book

Also available from us courtesy of Oxford University Press:
Young Readers' Dictionary
(large print edition)
Young Readers' Thesaurus
(large print edition)

For further information or a free brochure, please contact us at:
Ulverscroft Large Print Books Ltd.,
The Green, Bradgate Road, Anstey,
Leicester, LE7 7FU, England.
Tel: (00 44) 0116 236 4325
Fax: (00 44) 0116 234 0205

MYSTERY AT MORWENNA BAY

Christina Garbutt

Budding criminologist Ellie is glad to help her gran recuperate after an accident, expecting to spend a quiet month in rural Wales before heading back to London to submit her PhD. But she's bemused to find that she's something of a celebrity in the village, and expected to help solve a series of devastating livestock thefts for which there is no shortage of suspects. She's also wrong-footed by the friendly overtures of handsome young farmer Tom — even though a relationship is absolutely the last thing she wants or needs . . .

JEMIMA'S NOBLEMAN

Anne Holman

1816: When her father's famous fan shop in the Strand is reduced to ashes, Jemima dons the clothing of a maid and moves with him to the docklands of London — and is present at an accident where William, Earl of Swanington, almost literally falls into her lap! But William is fleeing from accusations that he's murdered a servant — and when he sees the beautiful Jemima at a Society ball, he wonders if she's the one who robbed him after his accident! Can true love blossom in such circumstances?

CHRISTMAS DOWN UNDER

Alan C. Williams

Australia, 1969: Manchester lass Pamela has given life in Sydney as a Ten Pound Pom a fair go, but since her husband ran off with a younger woman, she longs to return to the UK. However, when she books a one-way flight to take herself and her four-year-old daughter Sharon home by Christmas, it appears fate has other ideas. As Pamela's festive project at work takes off and she meets gorgeous but fashion-challenged teacher Nick, she begins to wonder whether life in Australia has more to offer than she'd thought . . .

CHRISTMAS GHOSTS AT THE PRIORY

Fenella J. Miller

Miss Eloise Granville is begrudgingly accepting of her arranged marriage to Viscount Garrick Forsythe — but when she discovers he is not aware of her infirmity, she is horrified. The wedding is only three weeks away, and it's far too late to cancel. Will he think he has been tricked? As Eloise anxiously awaits Garrick's arrival at St Cuthbert's Priory, the resident ghosts learn of the betrothal and unleash a fury that puts them both in grave danger. Will they find love amidst the chaos, or will circumstances push them apart?

THE RAGS OF TIME

Pamela Kavanagh

Escaping an emotionally unbearable life with her husband, Hannah flees with her young daughter to the town of Malpas, where she hopes to uncover her family's past and build a new life. Arriving with no wedding ring and baby Vinnie tucked under her shawl, Hannah struggles to find a place to stay. As nightfall approaches, she stumbles across a cottage owned by kindly Widow Nightingale, who takes them in — but will Hannah be able to find work, build a stable life for her daughter, and discover happiness in the town?